Travers Corners

Travers Corners

Scott Waldie

Lyons & Burford, Publishers

To my wife JANE; *daughter* BROOKE; *son* TIM; *mom* SWEDE;
and my oldest and best friend FRANK COLWELL
—thanks for the leeway.

Printed in the United States of America

10 9 8 7 6 5 4 3 2

Design by Jennifer Corsano

Library of Congress Cataloging-in-Publication Data

Waldie, Scott.
Travers Corners / Scott Waldie.
p. cm.
Contents: From the diary of Traver C. Clark—Travers Corners—Word gets around—Heaven is a river—Quintin—Three yahoos—Pastime—Travels—D. Downey.
ISBN 1-55821-533-6
1. Montana—Social life and customs—Fiction. 2. City and town life—Montana—Fiction. I. Title.
PS3573.A42137T7 1997
813′.54—dc20 96-34406 CIP

Abridged versions of "Heaven Is a River" and "Pastime" have appeared in *Sporting Classics* and *Gray's Sporting Journal*, respectively.

CONTENTS

Acknowledgments

JIM AND PAM Pappenfus, Ridge and Marjorie Harlan, Frances, Millie Narancich, the Dogs, Aunt Dora, Uncle Howard, Clark, Doug Booth, Tom Morgan, Bruce Beithon, Glenn Brackett, Dolly and Alan Carroll, Jeff and Patty Walker, Bob Kaufman, Dr. Stan Wilson, Joe Munroe, Russel Chatham, Tom McGuane, Marnie Pavelich, Nick and Ann Novich, C. L. and Connie Clark, Miss Winnerah of M. H. Stanley School—wherever you are, Bruce Reeves, Dr. Norman Shumway, and a very special thank you to Dick Lower.

Prologue

ENTERING TRAVERS CORNERS, Montana, where nothing much has happened since Herbert Hoover stopped for gas; where if it weren't for rumors there would be little news at all; and where large trout—no, better than large trout, fictitious trout—await the angler. The angler, of course, is responsible for his own luck and timing, and he must, as with everything in life, leave the rest to chance.

1

~

From the Diary of Traver C. Clark

SEPTEMBER 28TH, 1873:

I have spent most of the morning catching up with my journal. Albie was up early and has made a camp with a sense of permanence about it, a welcome awakening as we have been traveling hard this last week. The horses are in need of rest. D. Downey has gone fishing and I plan to hike into the Elkheart Mountains.

I spent the afternoon sketching, my feet dangling from the edge of a rock cliff a thousand feet above the valley floor. The Elkhearts towered above me another five thousand feet. From there I could follow the red of D. Downey's mackinaw as he weaved at a fisherman's pace along the river. I watched Albie tend to the camp for a few hours, then he rode east in search of game. We are eight days north of the newly established Yellowstone Park.

The valley is small, perhaps thirty miles long and about ten miles wide. Its size seems inviting after the vastness of the Yellowstone. The Elkheart River flows north, and from this afternoon's vantage point I could clearly see the tributary that joins the river across from our camp.

Mountains, sweeping and wooded to the south and the east, violently jagged to the west. Rolling hills and distant ranges give the valley its northern border. The beauty of this valley—well, there aren't any words for it, so I won't even try. But, simply put, it is the most incredible place I have ever seen.

Tonight, over an entree of Partridge à la Albie and the remaining stores of our liquor, we were in agreement: this campsite was the most spectacular since we left Jackson's Hole (which will be a month ago tomorrow). An indescribable beauty, or so I thought, but D. Downey, after a considerable portion of the whiskey, seemed to sum it up quite well.

"According to the good book, it took six full days for God to create the heavens and the earth. But, I would wager, He did the whole job in five. Then, on the sixth day He got up early, and He worked late, and He gave this little valley His undivided attention, before He rested on the seventh."

It was the bonniest place D. Downey had seen since he left Berwick-on-Tweed and tears welled up in his eyes. "Sor-r-ry, boys," he explained, "but I always get all waxed and lyrical when I think aboot the heather."

Albie, a man who has trapped nearly everywhere in the Rockies, was even more succinct, "Purdiest country I ever did see. Makes a feller feel all powdered up inside his head; makes a feller wanna spit whiskey."

Tomorrow, D. Downey and I plan to do some fishing up on Carrie Creek. And, here, dear diary, I must report on some indulgences: earlier this evening, as the sun was taking its leave, it lit an aspen grove above the stream flowing in across the river. The gold of the leaves reminded me of Carrie. If hair could be seasonal, then Carrie's would be autumn, and I said as much to D. Downey. He agreed, saying that would be a good name—Carrie Creek.

Albie then informed us that very few places had names in the Elkheart, other than the river and the mountains. "Go ahead," he said, "name 'er Carrie Creek, the name jest might stick."

With that, I fear, I jarred the lid to Pandora's box, and before we could put our humilities in check, we had come into the valley over Albie Pass, we are camped in the shadow of Mt. D. Downey, and, I am embarrassed to report, this last entry is being written from the floor of Travers Valley.

September 29th:

We have voted to stay here on the Elkheart for an additional four days; then we must be pushing on if we want to make our stage out of Missoula. In a few more weeks: D. Downey will be back logging in Denver and chasing the "ladies" at O'Malley's; Albie will be holed up for the winter somewhere in Idaho; and I will be back under the intolerable and suffocating wing of the family and Clark Industries.

What an unlikely trio we are: D. Downey, a full-blooded Scot; Albie, whose blood is a mixture of French and Nez Perce; and me, the blue blood from Boston.

So many times this trip I have thought of selling my shares in the company. I could liquidate and be back in Denver in the spring and marry Carrie. I am aware that if I sell all my holdings in such a short time, I will realize only half their value; but then half of a vast fortune is still a tidy sum.

I wish Carrie were here to see all of this. Perhaps I should start a ranch somewhere in Montana. No, not somewhere, but right here.

2

~

Travers Corners

Now, if you were to read on in Traver's journal, you would learn that he went on to live out his dream. He traveled back to Boston that fall, he did sell his shares in the family business, he did go back to Denver and marry Carrie, and he did return to the Elkheart Valley to start the Carrie Creek Cattle Company. The Clark family history from that point on, and I'll try to be brief, goes as follows . . .

Things went well those first years, Carrie Creek was one of the largest ranches in Montana's history—that is, until the killing winter of 1888. Carrie Creek lost its entire herd. Traver went from cattle baron to struggling rancher. In order for his family to survive, for he and Carrie had two boys by then, he had to sell most of Carrie Creek. The following year they lost one of their sons—I forget his name just now—to pneumonia, leaving only Ethan.

In 1925 Carrie died, and in the spring of the following year Traver followed her. By then the town of Travers Corners had sprung up, and the original Carrie Creek homestead, once an outpost in the wilderness, found itself just on the outskirts of town. The name Travers Valley never did catch on, but the town was named for him. However, the other two names from that campsite did stick just as Albie said they might—you still come into the Elkheart Valley over Albie Pass, and Mt. D. Downey still shadows the valley.

Ethan, along with his wife, Anna, and their four children, kept Carrie Creek alive, and though the 4C brand no longer grazed over an empire, it did manage to prosper some. Then, keeping with his father's timing in investments, Ethan decided that the fall of 1929 was as good a time as any to get bullish in the market.

Well, that financial move cost them the rest of the ranch. Ethan managed to hang onto the ranch house and a couple of acres. Once their children had grown and gone, he and Anna converted the old log home, and Carrie Creek became Clark's Boarding House. They took in boarders there until the early '50s. Ethan passed on in '51, Anna lived on until '61. I knew them both. Fine people. Good friends.

After Anna died, the old home sold several times; then in 1968 it caught fire and burned to the ground, all except the carriage house.

Scott could have told all of this to you himself, but he called me in just to get you acquainted with Travers Corners; me being the valley's oldest resident. Ninety-four next November. Oh, I'm sorry—been rattling on and didn't get around to introducing myself. Charlie, Charlie Miller's my name. Been in the Elkheart for a long time. Taught school around here for fifty-seven years. History teacher.

I knew Traver. I was just a boy, but I remember him.

Anyway, back to the carriage house. Back in 1973 the great-grandson of Traver Clark, Judson C. Clark—Jud—who was born and raised right here in Travers, bought the old carriage house and he turned it into the Carrie Creek Boat Works and Guide Service. People around here just call it the Boat Works; well, you wouldn't want to say The Carrie Creek Boat Works and Guide Service any more times than you would have to.

Scott also asked me if I wouldn't mind showing you around Travers—the locals just call the town Travers and tend to drop the Corners part. Well, it would be my pleasure.

I decided to start this tour right here where Traver, Albie, and D. Downey camped over one hundred years ago. Right across from us is Carrie Creek coming into the Elkheart River. Pretty spot, isn't it? I favor this particular vantage point, because from right here, down in the willows and trees, everything looks like it must have looked to Traver when he camped here and wrote in his journals; probably sitting right about where you and I are standing.

As you can see, since that fall day in 1873, not much has really changed around Travers, I mean on the grand scale of change. Yes, journals have evolved into laptop computers, and sure, traveling by horseback has been replaced by interstates, but the wilderness can still be felt. Jud says it's because while the rest of the world has been rushing to own a condo overlooking the Global Village, the folks around Travers have dug their heels into the time continuum, and are trying to keep everything the same as it was in 1956. For the most part they've been successful, because the town looks much the same as it did forty years ago. The population then was 212, today it's 317. If you follow me over to that clearing you'll be able to see the rooftops of Travers. Careful walking through here—the ground's a little slippery after last night's rain. Just through the willows, there, you can make out the Boat Works on the hill above town. Jud's been remodeling the old carriage house for over twenty years, and the people around town don't really expect to see its completion, but Jud's gaining on it.

Anyway, let's take a walk into town. Scott wanted me to introduce you to the key characters in Travers.

Well, let's see, I told you about how the town got its name, at least the Travers part, but I didn't tell you about how the Corners came about, did I? Can't remember if I did or not. Hell to be old. Anyways, Travers was the crossroads for the old Yellowstone and Missoula stage lines and that's why they added the Corners. Better watch your step walking through this field, the Morgans had their bulls in here last week.

We'll take this shortcut through Lee Wright's back yard. That's Lee over there mowing his lawn. Now, we'll just go up the alley here and we're out on Main Street.

The great thing about a small town like Travers is that I can show you the scenic route as well as take you on the business loop, and we won't even have to step from this curb. So, here it goes—Travers Corners—left to right, and it won't take long:

Now, straight across from us, on the other side of First Street, that's McCracken's General Store. One-stop shopping at McCracken's, but not because they have everything you need, but because it's the *only* place to stop and shop in Travers. Been owned by the McCracken family since 1947. Junior McCracken runs it now. Inside you'll find: horseshoes to notions, baling twine to clock radios, groceries, stationery, some car parts, plumbing and electrical supplies, hardware and lumber; and knowing Junior's merchandising skills you are likely to find the above items down the same aisle. McCracken's fills all your medical needs as Junior is the town's pharmacist. It's the local post office as well, and Junior's wife, Pam, is the Postmistress. In addition to all that, if you want to buy yourself some whiskey, you pick it up at the general store, as McCracken's is also the State Liquor Store. You can rent videos, pick up a copy of the daily paper, buy a new paperback. I guess if it's possible for Travers to have a cultural hub it would have to be the old general store.

Junior loves to hunt birds and fish; fortunately for the aforementioned, he is in no danger of shooting anything or catching anything. But, in spite of his failures on field and stream, he remains the optimist, always in a good mood, and he's been that way since he was born. I taught history to him. He was one of those kids with his head always buried in a book, a slide rule or two in his pocket.

The steeple you see over the roof of the general store belongs to the Baptist Church. The Methodists congregate over on Second Street and the Catholics have to motor their guilt thirty miles north to the town of Reynolds.

Right across Main Street you see the Tin Cup Bar and Cafe. It's owned by Sarah Easterly and her uncle Sal. Sarah does the cooking, Sal tends the bar. Good food. Stiff drinks. They moved here from New York City under some tough circumstances, about . . . mmm . . . fifteen years ago. Sarah's son and husband were killed, caught in crossfire of two warring gangs on a playground. They came here because they wanted to get as far away from the city, every city, as they possibly could. Travers was just what they were looking for. They're good people. You're going to like them. Sal's from the Bronx. He's a character.

On the opposite corner sits the old stage depot. Beautiful isn't it? The rock work and timbers. It's designated as a Historical Landmark by the state. Nowadays, the town's offices and library are on the first floor. Oh, and by the way, Traver's original journals are on display inside the library, so while you're in town you might want to stop and see them. Traver kept his diary until his death and you can buy copies of it from the library. Excerpts from the journals have been reprinted in the state's history books.

On the second floor is the Elkheart Medical Clinic—Doctor Thomas Higgins in residence. Well, he's in residence unless it's a Tuesday or a Thursday. Doc goes fishing on Tuesdays and Thursdays.

He came to the valley nearly forty years ago, as a young G.P. on a fishing trip. He met Sally Wendall. They were married and Doc stayed. Raised four sons here in the valley. All fine men. He can fix bones, deliver babies, and take out a gallstone. If the community has a cornerstone, or a sage, it would be the Doc. His shingle reads, DR. THOMAS HIGGINS, GENERAL PRACTITIONER OF MEDICINE, but everyone in Travers calls him Doc out of respect. He could have practiced anywhere in the country but he chose to be a general practitioner in Travers. He attributes this decision to his dedication to medicine, and the great dry fly waters found in the Elkheart Valley, not necessarily in that order.

Next door to the depot is the bank, Webb's Insurance next to it, then the Roxy Theater. The old home with the red roof is our local real estate. Down there a couple of blocks, at the end of town, past the houses, that's the Take 'er Easy Motel—clean, comfortable.

Now, if you look down the highway about a mile, you can just make out the old train station. See it? Here, stand over here. Trains don't come through Travers anymore—sure do miss 'em.

Coming back up this side of Main, you have Dolores's Hair Salon. Dolores, she's a caution, that one. What a beauty she was when she was young, and she still has her way with the men. I might be old, but she is the kind of woman who can bring back the memories to a man. If you know what I mean? She was in the same class as Jud and Henry, and I'll tell you about Henry in a moment.

Well, that brings us around to where we stand, except for right behind us—that's Ed's Chevron. Ed's a good mechanic, if you ever need one. Unless, of course, you are driving an import. Ed doesn't work on imports, and it's not for his lack of knowledge, mind you; it's a matter of patriotism with Ed.

Oh, and if you'll turn around and look back over Town Bridge and the river, you'll be able to see the grandstands and fairgrounds, and our Little League baseball diamond.

So, let's walk on up to the Boat Works, the Boat Works being the main reason Scott has invited you into these pages. It's just a couple of blocks from here, as the crow flies, right up there on the hill, behind that stand of lodgepoles.

Now, about Henry Albie—Henry is the great-grandson of the man known as Albie in the journals, and Henry and Jud are best friends. Been best friends since they were kids. Like I say, I taught school; taught the two of them; and a pair of hellions they were, too, but likable hellions.

Henry can do just about anything, and it's a good thing, as doing the same thing day in and day out is not what Henry does best. You can imagine trying to teach him history. So, Henry shoes horses, guides fishermen for Jud, hires out as a ranch hand from time to time, has a working knowledge of just about everything with moving parts, and he plays the harmonica in a local country-and-western band.

Henry describes his marital status as "between marriages"; married

Dolores when they were still just kids, but it didn't last. He's a rounder, that one, likes his Jack Daniel's. He's one of the best fly fishermen I've ever seen.

He and Dolores are friends again, even see them out for a movie now and then. She lives in town. Henry lives out on the back road to Reynolds, just a few miles north of town. But, on weekends you're likely to see his pickup parked out back, and during the winter, it can be seen there for days on end. I think they have some kind of arrangement, if you know what I mean. That's Carrie Creek again running through town. Looks like the mayflies are out. Fishing will be good this afternoon, usually is after a little rain.

Whew, that hill never used to wind me! Hell getting old. Well, there it is, the old carriage house; now the Boat Works. The sign out front reads, CARRIE CREEK BOAT WORKS AND GUIDE SERVICE, JUDSON C. CLARK, PROPRIETOR. But Jud doesn't guide much anymore. Pulling on the oars at fifty isn't quite like it was twenty-five years ago. He still goes out, but only with old clients who have, over the years, become friends. He's got the driftboat business and that occupies him full time these days. People come from all over to get one of his dories. If you want one, you'll be years getting it as Jud's boats are all handmade and his are the only hands making them.

Jud's been remodeling this place forever, but, as you can see, it is no small building; two stories and a belfry. You don't see logs that size anymore. It housed the buckboards, tack, buggies, and cook wagons. Remember, Carrie Creek was a ranch covering 175,000 acres; had fifty men working on her. Anyway, the carriage house was long abandoned and about to fall down when Jud bought her.

You'll notice that the belfry has been refurbished and windowed in. Jud now calls it The Observatory and from up there you can see Travers, the river, all the way to Albie Pass; and at night you can see the glow of Reynolds. You get up to it by climbing a spiral staircase that is made entirely of old wagon parts, and it was projects like the staircase that have made the restoration go so slowly. I mean restoration goes slow when it's done by anyone, but when it's done by Jud it approaches geologic time. Jud brings new meaning to the word slow. Doc says Jud reminds him of a man who was sent for but couldn't get there. He walks slow, he talks slow, he's never on time to anywhere. Now, you would expect movements that were precise and measured in a craftsman, and Jud is a craftsman. But, he is also a dreamer, and when you couple precision with dreams, you don't get someone who dreams precisely, but someone who is slow.

He was like that in school, always gazing out the window, but still got the grades—even received a scholarship to U.C. Berkeley in Forestry. He left for college in the '60s. Well, the '60s being the '60s, and Berkeley being Berkeley, young people were changing directions, and he spent the second half of the decade there: two years studying forestry, two years studying eastern religions, six months studying with a Navajo shaman, and six months he's not sure of.

Spent some years traveling. Saw a lot of the world, working as he went.

Now, Jud's back home, building driftboats. He rarely travels farther than Reynolds, helps Sal coach Little League, and still manages to get in what he refers to as "medicinal amounts" of fishing. He was married once; it didn't work out. Says he's still looking. He's good friends with Sarah Easterly. The town gossips think they might be more than just good friends, but it's not true. I know them both real well, and that's just what they are—good friends.

Well, that wraps up the tour of Travers. Oh, there is one more thing Scott wanted me to tell you. These forthcoming stories were twenty years in the gathering; and not told in any specific order. They are, for the most part, inventions of Scott's imagination, and any similarity between the fictitious characters depicted in the following narratives and anyone living is purely intentional.

Hope you enjoy your time while you're in the Elkheart Valley, and maybe I'll bump into you again during your stay.

3

~

Word Gets Around

TRAVERS CORNERS, LIKE most small towns, has no newspaper, no radio station; so when what little news, good or bad, does come to town, it can be spread only by word of mouth. Many consider it their civil obligation to pass anything newsworthy along to their neighbors; and there are others who would call this gossip. But, you have to remember that gossip is the messenger to rumor, and when rumor becomes truth it becomes history; that is, of course, if it was juicy enough gossip to begin with.

Gossip usually begins as gospel, then graduates through the requisite stages of hearsay: exaggeration, both levels, gross and slight; embellishment; and misrepresentation. Seldom does it ever enter the realm of the out-and-out lie. What saves rumor from blatant prevarication is that somewhere, nestled deep down, at the very kernel of the canard, is the nucleus of truth. Unless, of course, the rumor is centered on trout fishing; where the requisite—and sometimes slow—stages of hearsay are brushed aside in favor of immediate mendacity.

The speed at which a story travels depends upon content. This was the rarest of rumors: it was *good* news traveling like wild fire. But, before it was rumor it was truth, and the following is how it happened. . . .

Jud couldn't remember a finer morning in May. The day had started with a series of events, which he elected to read as signs. The signs interpreted independently were not portentous, but collectively they came to him as an omen. First—it was warm, uncommonly warm for spring, the kind of day that might make a man think of fishing.

The second sign came as he looked out from the Boat Works window to see what at first he thought to be a mist over the Elkheart River. But this mist lifted, then it fell, only to lift again. He then realized that it wasn't a mist at all, but clouds: billowing swarms of mayflies, their countless wings catching the early light in a dazzling dance. *Ephemerella* Suite. Now Jud was actively thinking about fishing.

Downstairs, the third sign was much more subtle and probably would have been missed by anyone not already looking for an excuse to get out on the river. Annie the Wonderlab, easily the planet's smartest Labrador, sensing something was in the air, was unusually happy to see him. It was more than her typical morning milk-bone happy. She was prancing and whirling about. Her tail slapped against a broom leaning in the corner, causing it to fall against the standing hat rack and to knock but one hat free from the many cocked upon its branches. The hat, his fishing hat, rolled over to his feet. It could only have been taken as prophecy.

"Do you want to go fishing?" he asked. Those were the magic words. Annie barked and twirled her tail in response.

"I'll take that as a yes. Okay let's go. Go get in the boat." Annie was out the screen door and, after a quick pee and a good long roll in the grass, performing her usual lablutions, she leaped into the already trailered driftboat. Jud gathered the needed belongings and his fishing gear, then hitched the *S.S. Lucky Me* to the Willys and drove to the put in at the West Fork Bridge.

The day ahead of him was one he had done many times before and it would follow a certain pattern. There was one riffle just upstream from the bridge, which he always fished, by tradition, before floating on down the river.

With the dory tied to a stump and bobbing in a backwater, Jud was now wading his way up to that riffle with Annie half-swimming and half-walking alongside him in the current. Long and lean, he moved slowly in the current, but then Jud moved slowly out of the current. In his thirties, his movements were those of a much older man. Some viewed his slow, almost underwater pace, his seemingly weightless gait, as the quiet and easy ways of a craftsman. Others, and those who knew him best, knew Jud as a man who was born to dawdle. He was a natural. He could linger with the best of them; a kind man and a dreamer; a world-class procrastinator; and a perfectionist about his craft. These were the characteristics that protracted everything about him. These were the elements that meant if you ordered one of his driftboats today, you would get it in two years. His dories were widely recognized as well worth the wait.

It was a perfect morning, barely a breeze, and warm. The leaves on the cottonwoods, having leafed out only the week before, seemed surreal—bright green with white undersides gently twisting on the wind, flashing their reflections across the Elkheart's still-clear water, spangling like a million tambourines in the early morning light. "The river won't look like this tomorrow," he said, scratching Annie behind the ear. "This weather will bring the thaw to the high country, and by tonight she'll be running high and muddy."

He took one more look around and sighed from satisfaction. "That's what's so great about spring, Annie-girl—You think you can remember what it looks like, but you can't, and every year it bowls you over." Then he stripped off some line, pausing for a moment to smile at Annie, who was now in position, sitting on the shore, ears up at full alert, staring into the river, waiting impatiently for Jud to hurry up and make his cast. So he did just that.

His first cast was one of those warm-up, just-getting-a-little-line-out casts; a careless, casual, nonchalant, practice-swing cast. A cast made without looking as Jud was still staring at the riverscape, and beyond to the Elkheart Range, and at Mt. D. Downey still draped in snow.

His fly wasn't fifteen feet in front of him when the fish took. Being the more alert of the two, Annie spotted the rise before he did, and was already heading into the water by the time Jud was conscious that a fish was on—a rainbow trout, a very small one, and nothing to be excited about. Annie, however, treated every trout Jud caught with the same enthusiasm, and as soon as any fish was caught, she was right there at his side, excitedly waiting for their fish to be landed. She looked at it as her fish, too. The trout, no longer than five inches, was quickly in. It was hooked well and Jud kneeled down into the river to remove the hook and release his catch. With her nose no more than inches from his hands, Annie looked in, assessing the size of the fish. She then shot Jud an incredulous look that read just as clearly as if it had been spoken, "Well, we'll have to do better than that, won't we?"

"Don't give me that," Jud defended himself, "that fish fooled you as well. You came running down here like I had just hooked into a monster. But who am I talking to? Aren't you the same Labrador that greets every squirrel that comes into our yard like it's a surprise visit from the Islamic Jihad?" He splashed water at her with a cupped hand. She barked back. He stood up laughing and readied his next cast as Annie returned to her spot, ready for more action—larger action, she hoped.

Once again he stripped line from his reel, but before he could make another cast, Annie began barking furiously, and uncharacteristically left her appointed station. The object of her distraction was something large and shiny and it was tumbling toward him; a broad silver glare rolling along the bottom. First, he thought it to be a piece of tinfoil folding in the current; but as the form came closer, he recognized the distinct shape, and the sight took his breath. He reached for his net, stepped into the object's path, blocking it with his legs, and netted it—tucking his rod under his arm, since he needed the use of both hands. A giant rainbow trout. A mammoth fish. The size of fish you only see in the magazines, public aquariums, and dreams.

Jud went to the shore and spilled the great trout out on the bank. He placed his net over the fish, knowing the net to be twenty-four inches; and using it as a measure, he aligned the handle's end with the tip of the great trout's tail. She was five or six inches longer than the basket. "Whoa, Annie, that is some kind of fish! It *must* weigh fourteen or fifteen pounds, maybe sixteen pounds!"

She was dead, but only dead by moments as her silver still glistened, the intensity of her red markings still held their integrity, and her great broad back was still distinctly brindled in greens and blacks. "No hook marks or scars, Annie girl. Looks like she just rolled over and died of old age," he explained with a note of sadness in his voice—sad because this wonderful fish, this trout of such incredible beauty, had to die; and sad because he never had and never would catch such a fish. It was a perfect fish. A perfect shape. Jud and the Wonderlab watched as the trout's colors began to fade.

The sound of a truck coming over the bridge shook Jud from his amazement. It was Red Peterson pulling a six-horse trailer. Red, recognizing the boat, and then spotting Jud kneeling on the bank, rolled to a stop and hollered down to him. "How's the fishing, Jud?" The horses were shifting about in the trailer and their heavy footsteps rumbled on the bridge and echoed off the water.

Jud looked over to Annie and the smirk born of a practical joke crossed his face. He held up the trout.

"O-o-o-o-ooweee," yelled Red. "How big is she?"

"About fourteen pounds," then the prankish urges subsided and Jud shouted out the truth and the details. "A big rainbow. I thought I was dreaming but it just came floating by dead. Still had all its color." The bay mare, the last horse in the trailer, was never one that liked to be transported, and she was moving and beginning to kick. Her raucous stirrings garbled Jud's reply, but Red got the gist of it.

He went on his way, as Jud put the rainbow in the cooler, first to unload his horses, then on into town—where he stopped at McCracken's to pick up some medications for his wife.

The rumor had legs.

As you probably know, the best way to be a party to rumor is by eavesdropping, so listen in as the gossip begins, when Red tells Junior McCracken exactly what he had just witnessed as he was crossing the Elkheart . . .

Junior was at the back of the pharmacy when Red walked up. "Hi there, Red. Got your pills right here," Junior greeted him, dropping a pill container into a small white sack.

"I just saw Jud fishin' out at West Fork Bridge. I stopped and asked him how the fishin' was and he holds up this trout. I swear to God, Junior, that fish was a yard long. I asked him what kind of trout it was and how big. 'Rainbow,' he said, and I am pretty darn sure he said 'about nineteen pounds.'"

Junior was taking the news as well as could be expected, as Junior had never in his life caught such a fish. Jud was always catching bigger trout than Junior, but then anyone who fishes around Travers usually catches bigger trout than Junior. He was a slight shade of green, and his voice cracked as he went right to the most important question of the moment, now that the size had been established, "Did you happen to ask Jud what he caught it on?"

"I ain't too sure what he said, on accounta the horses were actin' up, 'cause of the heat and all, twistin' around in the trailer and makin' quite a racket. I am purty sure he said caught it on a streamer on a floatin' line, lots of lead; then he said somethin' about the color, but I couldn't hear him. I would'a run down there myself to git a closer look, but I had a bay mare in tow who was jest about to kick me out a new trailer door. Now, I ain't a-kiddin' you, Junior, it was the biggest fish I ever did see come outta the Elkheart or anywhere else for that matter."

Now, this was the kind of news Junior had to share with nearly everyone who came into McCracken's. He recounted the story, just as he heard it, remiss only in not mentioning the fact that Red couldn't really hear Jud clearly because of the horses.

So, now the rumor was only secondhand and already completely distorted. The great rainbow, the species being the only truthful portion of the gossip, had grown from "about fourteen pounds" to "'about nineteen pounds.'" And, "I thought I was dreaming . . . floating by . . . dead . . . still had all its color," had transformed into "'I caught it on a streamer . . . a floating line . . . lots of lead . . . and something about color.'"

A nineteen-pound rainbow, to anglephile and non-fisherman alike, is newsworthy; and the gossip spread, moving along, changing by embellishment as it was passed from messenger to messenger. But, it is in the angler's nature, when passing along a piscatorial tale, to enhance it. Anglers simply cannot resist making a good fishing story even better.

Through the Tin Cup Bar and Cafe, over to Ed's Garage, around the library, up to the Medical Clinic and certainly at McCracken's General Store, the story was being told and retold, circulating fast, but circulating slower than some rumors. This was for two reasons: one, it was good news, which, as we all know, travels slowly; and two, the rumor centered on fly fishing and this kind of news holds little interest for most women. Fishing will never be a major topic at Dolores's Hair Salon, and when you drop Dolores and her patrons from the rumor mill, the speed of any hearsay is much more than halved.

The rumor lost all touch with reality. By the time the news of Jud's fish reached the outlying ranches, and Henry Albie, later that afternoon, it had long left the world of mere gossip and rumor. It had graduated quickly from fishing story to fishing tale and was destined to be a yarn; and the fish could be fable by nightfall. Henry heard it from Mike, the UPS man, that Jud had caught a giant brown trout, maybe a new state record, twenty-something pounds, on a small dry fly and two-pound test.

Henry was going to town anyway. He and Dolores were going to the Tin Cup for a steak. So, he would stop by the Boat Works and get the straight skinny from Jud. Henry knew Travers. He knew the rumor mill. He also knew from a lifetime of fishing the Elkheart that, while such fish did live in the river, one of them is caught only when the moon is blue—and *never* on a dry fly.

The rumor had an entire afternoon to be passed around and exaggerated. Jud was out on the river, at the oars, drifting along, oblivious to the news that had swept town. Annie was in her usual spot, aft, on duck patrol. She came about the name Wonderlab not for her prowess in the field, since Jud didn't hunt; it was for her keenness streamside that she earned the epithet. Annie loved to fish. When their fishing was brisk, Annie was right by his side, moving quietly, never spooking a fish. She would delight in Jud's catch as though she had thrown the fly herself. When the fishing was slow she would be downstream, in the deep pools snapping at the whitefish rises.

Rowing the boat to shore, Jud was now stopping to fish the Buick Hole before taking out at Miller's Bend. Shipping the oars, Jud was already out of the boat, as was Annie. He pulled the dory onto the rocks and watched the water stream off the blades of his oar, catching the light as if it were crystal.

The Buick Hole isn't a hole really, but more of a side channel created by driftwood and a 1949 Roadmaster. That car had come to rest here one Saturday night many years ago when an overserved cowboy took the corner leading onto the bridge on two wheels, missing the bridge entirely but hitting the river dead on. The cowboy survived but the car wasn't seen again until the next summer and low water.

When river conditions are perfect—that would be when the water level is six inches below the decorative exhaust ports on the Roadmaster's front fender—an angler can get a drift on his fly right over where the back seat used to be, or there about, and take a fish from the sunken trunk. The water conditions were perfect.

As a boy, Jud would bicycle from town, down the old highway, now crumbling past repair in the shadows along the far bank, to fish the Buick

Hole with worms. The place always brought about memories of Henry, Donny, and himself as boys, with Junior McCracken tagging along. Here he was wading over the same rocks, to fish the same spot in the same way he did thirty-five years ago; and that, he thought, might be the secret to fishing—to wade the river as a man, while never forgetting to fish it as a child.

There were no fish rising, but he would fish the spot anyway—out of tradition. The fishing had been slow all day. He thought about the rainbow in the cooler as he moved into position downstream of the car. The stories he could tell about how he *landed* her. Dozens of ways crossed his mind, from midge to mouse, streamer to nymph. He'd decided on a nymph story, with a fine tippet. He thought the rainbow should have jumped five, no, make it nine times. He'd make the fight twenty minutes; no, fifteen; no, half an hour. But any story he could have made up wouldn't match some of the ones that were now being passed as the truth up and down the valley. Shrugging his shoulder and smiling, he knew all his fabrications would be for naught. Henry or Sarah would need only one look at him to see he was lying. But, he was going to do it anyway—just for the laughs.

He'd been on the river all day with hardly a rise save the whitefish. Annie, fed up with his performance all afternoon, wasted little time and went directly to the nearest pool to snap at the whities.

His first cast went too far to the left. He cast again, still not quite right. The third time was dead on. Landing just above the moss-covered portholes, his fly, a Cahill, took a feathered tumble across the seams of jagged light that edged the rear window of the Roadmaster. A quick mend, and then another, as it caught the crease of current and slack water. The mends held the fly for that single moment needed to attract a trout. Dancing and juddering, the fly was held in a watery suspension, balancing on the current line, right above the backseat, for seconds.

The silvered flash came from the dark water, from deep within the Buick, and took the Cahill. Feeling its sting, the fish leaped from the trunk, over the exposed fender, and into the fast water. The trout jumped and turned in the current. It looked like a rainbow. It then started pulling its way back into the wreckage, fighting Jud's line and looking for a wrap on a spring or an axle.

Annie, aware something was happening, was swimming her way upstream.

The fish was good-sized, fifteen inches, and scrappy, but Jud had the angle on him. The trout fought a hard and long fight, but then, after a short run, and one more jump, he tired and was being guided to the net. Annie was at his side. "Yep, about fifteen inches, wouldn't you say, girl?" She stopped her panting long enough to bark her approval.

Cradling the brown trout in his hands, holding it just beneath the surface, he marveled at the unusual markings, so silvery, so lightly colored for a brown trout. He thought he was fighting a rainbow the whole time; in fact, he was sure of it—until the fish slipped over the edge of his net. Even the brown's large black spots were muted, almost a gray. He thought again of the rainbow in the cooler and worked on his story quickly once more. *Caught it on Hare's Ear nymph . . . jumped twelve times . . . took me forty-five minutes to land her.* That was his story and he was going to stick to it for as long as his straight face would hold.

The brown was regaining its senses and lay in his hands barely touching them, its tail waving, almost blowing in the current like Wyeth's curtains. A twist of its body and the trout was free; a few shiny flickers, like sunlight through smoke, and it was gone.

Annie looked up and said without saying with her Labrador eyes, "Well, it's about time."

"All right, Annie, go get in the boat. Let's float on down to the bend. It's getting late."

Jud hadn't been back to the Boat Works but ten minutes when Henry and Dolores drove up the hill. Jud had just ducked inside the house with an armload of gear when he heard the sound of Annie's bark. She only gave it a bark or two as she quickly recognized it was Henry's truck coming. Most would think that she knew it was Henry's truck by the size and shape, but Jud contends that she does it by memorizing license plates. He looked out the kitchen window to see them getting out of the pickup. He hurriedly practiced his story. *Caught it on Hare's Ear nymph . . . jumped twelve times . . . took me forty-five minutes to land her.*

Smiling, he went out the back door. He couldn't wait to see the expression on Henry's face when he saw that fish. But, as he came around the corner of the kitchen, there was Henry stealing his moment. He had the cooler open and was holding the trout for Dolores to see. Sensing that his planned prevarication had already been compromised by Henry's getting to the trout before him, he all too impatiently rushed into his story; telling it as he crossed the yard, "Caught it on a Hare's Ear . . . jumped fourteen times, took me almost an hour to land it."

Henry laid the fish back in the ice, then stood up smiling. It was a faint smile, and his eyes, between blinks, held that quizzical look of disbelief. Jud knew the look and he knew what it meant: "Oh yeah, *sure* you did; now tell me another one." He'd known that look all his life. He knew it just as he knew his own face was giving way; he could feel it betraying him as he knew it would, and he started laughing.

"Okay. Okay," Jud said. "I found her dead. I was fishing down at West Fork Bridge, when I spotted something bright in the water. Annie spotted her first, really. I guess she just rolled over and died and was tumbling along in the current; still had most of her color."

"Yeah, we heard about the trout. Only by the time the word got to me, the fish was twenty pounds—and you had caught it on a dry fly."

"*What?* Got to *you?* How'd *you* hear about it?"

"Came in with the UPS guy."

"Well, how in the . . ."

"Jud, honey, that fish of yours has been the talk of Travers Corners all day," Dolores said in her usual flirtatious tones. "I heard it straight from Junior. He was tellin' everybody that went into McCracken's. Junior was so darned excited about it that you'd think he was the one who caught it." She laughed. "There was talk around that it might be a new state record."

"Don't think so," Henry guessed. "This fish wouldn't of weighed more than fourteen pounds. State record on a river rainbow is over twenty pounds. But this here trout jest might'a set a new *land-speed* record on the rumor mill. Where did Junior hear it?" Henry asked.

"Red Peterson," Dolores answered.

"Aaaah." Then Jud puzzled, "But I told Red what happened. He saw me hold out the fish. I told Red I found it dead."

"Well, the town took to Red's story," Dolores confirmed, " 'cause his story was a lot better."

"Confirming the old adage, better Red's than dead," Jud said smiling.

Dolores moaned. Henry rolled his eyes.

Dolores was ready for a night out, even though it was just down to the Tin Cup. "Okay, darling, you've seen your fish; now come on take me out to dinner. Then she put her arm through Jud's. "And you come, too, Jud, if you want. Sarah's cooking tonight." Dolores was looking her usual enticing self, dressed like Saturday night. Henry was dressed like a hired hand.

"Well, I . . ." Jud's answer was cut short by the sound of Doc's car coming up the drive. Annie didn't bark at all. She knew it was Doc's car by the sticky lifter.

The cooler was still open, and Doc was out of the car, going right to it.

"Hiya, Doc," Jud greeted, as did Henry and Dolores.

But Doc went right on by them and looked into the cooler. "Sweet Jesus Marie. Now *that's* a fish. And Junior said you caught it on a *streamer?*

"No, Doc, I found it . . ."

"She is such a beauty, isn't she? Just so perfectly shaped, isn't she? Don't think it was any nineteen pounds though, looks more like fifteen. But my God, what a fish. I've fished the Elkheart for forty years and never have I seen such a trout," Doc said pulling out his pipe and packing it with tobacco. "I am a little surprised though, Jud, knowing you, that you didn't release it."

"But Doc, I'm telling you, I found the fish dead."

"Dead? Junior McCracken swore to me that you caught it on a streamer."

"No, what happened was . . ."

Dolores could see the fish story coming—only this time in detail; it's the details in a fishing story that lead to more fishing stories. She'd seen it too many times before. She was getting hungry. "Hey, Doc, we were all just goin' down to the Tin Cup," she interrupted. "Why don't ya come with us?"

"No thanks, Dolores, I have to get home. To tell you the truth I just hung around the clinic tonight and puttered around, kind of waiting for the light to come on up here at the Boat Works. I really wanted to see this fish . . . and hear all about it. Glad I did. She is such a rare and beautiful thing," he said wistfully, staring into the cooler. "Just sorry you didn't catch it, Jud, and sorrier still that I didn't catch it." Doc laughed, then his face went mockingly stern. "I am going to get that Junior McCracken. He's the perpetrator of this fraud, not Red Peterson. Red tells it like it is. Junior has a known tendency to tell it the way *he'd* like it to be.

"Well, gotta run. See you all later."

"Yeah, see ya, Doc."

But Doc stopped in his tracks and turned to ask: "Hey, Jud, what are you going to do with that fish?"

"Going to take it over to that guy in Helena. Have it mounted."

"Oh, that's good. I like that. A fish such as that should live on in some way."

After Doc had left, the three walked down the hill to the Tin Cup. The sun was setting and the air was cool. The cafe was empty, but the bar was unusually full for a weeknight. Everyone was asking about the fish; everyone was sorry to hear that Jud had found the fish dead.

Sarah cooked them their meals; then along with Sal, who got Eddy to pinch-hit for him behind the bar, she joined them for dinner. Sitting at the big table at the rear of the otherwise empty cafe, the five laughed as they relived the events of the day, and how the exaggerated tale of Jud's trout could be traced directly to Junior's totally unintentional untruth. They formed a pact. . . .

"I say we don't tell Junior the truth for a while," Jud said with a wry smile. "Let's keep up the lie for as long as we can, I mean just for Junior."

"Yeah, I like that," Henry said. "In fact I think it's only fittin'."

Sarah, Sal, and Dolores agreed and it was set: starting tomorrow they would all go into McCracken's at staggered times. They would all say they had seen the fish. They would all say that nineteen pounds was probably an underestimation for the rainbow. Jud coached his allies on what to say: "Caught it on Hare's Ear, jumped twelve times, took the better part of the afternoon to land."

"Junior's jealous of every fish caught that ain't at the end of *his* line, but a fish like *that* fish, he's gonna contort with envy," said Henry.

"We'll stew him in his own juices," Jud added with a Bogart lisp.

"Okay, Junior's got a little something coming back to him," Sarah agreed laughing, "but don't you two get mean."

"Sarah," Sal said, "da boys are right. Junior deserves to be ribbed a little bit, you know, a *piccolo scherzo*.

"*Piccolo scherzo*?"

"That's Italian for a little practical joke," Sarah explained. "A little revenge."

"Maybe we should wrap da fish in some-a newspaper. Leave it on his-a front-a step-a?" Jud said in his best Don Corleone Italian.

Sal, along with everyone else, laughed, but at the same time he was getting a little edgy to leave. Sal didn't fish and he bored quickly with fishing talk. What he couldn't understand the most is why anyone would talk about fishing when in the next room there was cold beer, a thirty-six-inch Sony, and the Dodgers against the Giants. Twilight doubleheader. That rookie kid named Hershiser who was throwing nothing but smoke was scheduled to pitch the second game. Sal was thinking about excusing himself, but first he had to ask, "And where is dat Junior, anyways? You'd think he would'a phoned or tracked Jud down by now, with da news of such a fish in town."

And where *was* Junior? That unwitting Junior McCracken, purveyor of gossip? Well, that would be Junior, the silhouette you see against the silvered water of sunset; fishing the large pool just below the West Fork Bridge; fishing a floating line and streamers with lots of lead; standing in cool water; casting into the shadows of the eternal river. And, with his luck, he'd be catching a few small ones or nothing at all. But, as he fishes in the beauty of Elkheart Valley, one with the river, the wildlife, the gentle sounds, the moist evening air, and all that surrounds him, with nothing but the rod and reel to fill his mind—how unlucky could he be?

Epilogue

Author's note: This is a story from twelve years ago, but Jud wanted me to let you know that just three years ago a rancher from Reynolds was introduced to him. Jud had never heard of the rancher, or of his ranch. But the rancher certainly had heard of Jud, had remembered Jud's name, and had remembered why. "Aren't you the guy that caught that twenty-pound rainbow a few years back?"

Rumors are born quickly but old ones die hard.

By the way, Annie the Wonderlab is still a wonder, but now a wonder because she can still make it from the kitchen to the living room on her very old Labrador legs. Since that day when they found the rainbow she has fished for whitefish hundreds of times and made thousands of snaps, but never caught one.

Jud thinks of that catch almost daily, since the great trout is beautifully mounted, three stories up in the observatory at the Boat Works. He remembers just as clearly the wonderful brown trout caught in the back of the Roadmaster; just as he remembers it to be the second-best time he's ever had in the backseat of a Buick.

4

~

Heaven Is a River

JUD WAS AT the rear of the Boat Works bent over one of his river dories.

It had been a long and quiet afternoon. In one hand he moved a small plane along the gunwales while the other hand followed, brushing away the oak shavings and checking his work. Stepping back from the boat, he tried to twist the day's kinks from his back. He shed his apron, adjusted his suspenders, and leaned against the workbench. The boat was far from finished; he was done for the day.

From there he looked north through the shop's windows to see a sky filled with threatening clouds, typical of late September storms; they didn't seem to roll in as much as they liked to bear down. The afternoon sun was making one last appearance from beneath the clouds, and its brilliance was made doubly harsh against the oncoming darkness. Walking over to the back door of the workshop, Jud laid his plane down and stood looking out on Travers Corners, awash in a low light of reds and yellows and edging the buildings and sidewalks that lined Main in a white neon.

He pulled a red bandana from his hip pocket and wiped the dust from his glasses, then wove his glasses back into place through his brown, giving way to gray, hair. His movements were slow and precise, befitting his trade. If his tired old clothes—flannel shirt, faded Levi's, vest, and moccasins—had the energy to make a fashion statement, you would have to read it in *Mother Earth News*. He pulled an old pocket watch from his vest—five twenty-five. Then holding the timepiece by its chain, he dropped it back into its pocket. Jud always imagined that time carried in a pocket watch might travel a little slower.

The sound of someone coming didn't interrupt Jud's weather watch, for on Friday afternoon, around quitting time, it could only be Henry.

Hobbling through the door, carrying a six-pack, Henry handed Jud a beer, and though complaint was not one of Henry's traits, today had been one of those days, and he was worried about tomorrow. With no hi or hello, he greeted Jud in his usual monotone, "How am I going to take anyone fishin' in this weather? 'Spose'ta be like this fer the next couple of days."

"What's with the limp?" Jud asked.

"Shoein' old man Kelly's mare this mornin' and she kicked me good right here on my leg," he answered, pointing to a place high on his thigh. "A couple of inches higher and you could call it my ass.

"Man, I'll be in great shape for rowin' tomorrow. 'Course if this rain keeps up there ain't gonna be any fishin' tomorrow. It drops a few more degrees out there and it's gonna snow. Man, I ain't ready for winter jest yet. Those folks I got will cancel sure."

Cracking open his beer, Jud leaned back, for just as he knew that complaining was rare for Henry, he also knew Henry wasn't done.

"I mean I could use a couple of days of guiding 'cause the shoein's been slow. I could use the bucks. Got my eye on that new saddle over at McCracken's. Hey, how about buildin' a fire in here? I been out in it since daybreak, and that wind out there comin' off the East Bench has been blowin' through me all day."

Henry's face, long as a hoe handle, had just recounted grievous personal injury and had predicted bad weather, bad fishing, and financial ruin without moving a wrinkle. His deadpan was divided by a mustache set over lips that never seemed to move. Henry was what Will Rogers described as a "close chewer and a tight spitter."

"You can relax about your guide trip," Jud said and helped Henry gather the shavings for kindling. The guy called this afternoon and said they were running a little late. Wanted me to call the Take 'er Easy and tell them to hold their room.

"Henry," said Jud with a sympathetic smile as he lit the fire and added kindling, "I think you could be in real trouble on this one. When I told this guy that the weather was a little iffy, he said"—then Jud mimicked a deep Texas accent—"he was 'gonna go fishin' come hell or high water.'"

"Then he asks me if it's all right if he brings his shotgun along tomorrow. I said there was no real reason to—waterfowl season's not starting for another month. He says it wouldn't be the first duck season that he'd opened up a little early.

"Then he puts his wife on. She wants to know if we have a vet in town. Seems her poodle has been getting carsick on all the windy roads."

"I suppose this fits right in there with bein' kicked by that mare," Henry said, grimacing. "What's their names? Where they from?"

"I never heard her name, but he's called Jimbo," Jud said almost apologetically. Jimbo Johnson from Houston. He's in oil."

"Bingo."

"I've got some good news, though," Jud quickly offered.

"Better'n rowing two Texicans and their poodle down the river in a rain storm. Jesus, I wish I were a little more flush. I'd call in sick."

"The Professor called. He'll be here this evening."

You would have to know Henry pretty well to be able to observe his change from despair to surprise; everything took place in his eyes. "Just showin' up ain't like the Professor."

"Yeah, I know, and listen to this: he's coming today, fishing tomorrow, and going back to Boston on Sunday. And he might be coming back in late October."

"Well," Henry said, shaking his head, "things must be pretty darn good in the teachin' business. He's been comin' out here like clockwork for . . . how long we been guidin' the Professor now?"

"Mmmm, seventeen years. But he always comes out in July. Said he was in need of an angling sabbatical. We've guided a lot of people over the years, but I suppose I like guiding the Professor the best—always learn something from him."

"Yep, he's one of the good ones alright. Hope he gits here soon; I gotta be gone by six-thirty."

As the fire warmed, they continued to talk about the Professor. An eavesdropper would soon have found out about the Professor's expertise with a dry fly, his love of the Elkheart River, his congenial manner, and his fondness for cognac. But there would be little chance they would learn, at least from these two, that the Professor, Dr. Clark Munroe, was one of America's foremost anthropologists, a man of letters, an admired author and lecturer, a man who traveled the world and took notes. The notes became studies, the studies became history. A fascinating man, a man who had called Margaret Mead "Maggie."

That was the Professor's other life, and Henry and Jud only knew him within the context of Montana, where he was a contrast to be sure, for he was all tweed, high brow, and upper crust in the land of down home, denim, and sourdough. Despite the differences, the Professor seemed to fit in quite well around Travers Corners, but that's the mark of a great anthropologist—to slip in and out of cultures without making a ripple.

It was six-thirty and still no Professor. "Guess I won't be seein' him this trip. Unless you can persuade him to come down and listen to the band tomorrow night? Oh," Henry added as he headed for the door, "Peggy Martin has got a sister visitin'. I hear she is real nice and fine lookin'."

"Henry, the Mama Juggs Band is not exactly the Professor's first choice in music. He's Mozart and Beethoven, Mama Juggs is Merle and Mo Bandy. You know how he feels about that kind of music."

"Well, give 'er a try," Henry said, then was out the door.

Two hours passed and Jud was back in the house; settled in at the fly-tying bench and just putting the whip finish to a Red Quill when headlights filled the room. Jud went to the back door to greet him. "Hello, Professor."

"And hello back to you, Jud," he said, coming through the screen door, shaking Jud's hand as he went. The Professor was not a tall man, but he attained the illusion of height by being lanky. In the light of the den Jud quickly saw a change in him. He was in his early seventies but never before had Jud seen his age. His walk had lost its nimble gait, but the blue eyes peering over a pair of half-glasses were as sharp as ever.

"What kept ya?" Jud asked.

"Oh, I am sorry. I know I'm late, but I have been working on a speech, believe it or not. I must have it prepared by Monday evening. The body of the speech came along quite easily, but I was having trouble with its closure. As I drove over Albie Pass I was privy to a most spectacular sunset, and it came to me—what better time to write a conclusion? So, I pulled over and penned an ending. Now I am unencumbered for the weekend. I have nothing more to do and nothing more on my mind than doing a little fishing. This weather is temporary, I hope?"

"Did you have supper?"

"Oh, I had plenty to eat on the plane." Then he got an almost sheepish grin. "I flew first class. I've always wanted to do that."

"Would you care for a beer or anything?"

"A beer sounds wonderful."

Handing him a beer, Jud tipped his own slightly. "Well good to have you back."

"Thank you. I do apologize for the short notice, but on Thursday evening it occurred to me that for the amount of time I was wasting thinking about coming here, I would surely save time and money in the long run by being here." He removed his bow tie. "Came right from school. Caught an eight-o'clock flight out of Boston." He pulled his pipe from his sport coat, which fit much the same as his slacks—loose almost to the point of looking borrowed.

"I've been dreaming about rainbows, Jud. La-a-arge rainbows."

"Good to hear you have been sleeping well, Professor."

"I only have but the one day. Where should we float?"

Large rainbow trout had narrowed it down in Jud's mind. Elkheart Canyon. "We'll float from the Gillespie Ranch down to the Widowmaker. There aren't near as many fish down there, but it's where the big ones pick up their mail."

"Is there any reason that we need to get away early?"

"No."

"Good. We septuagenarians have to offset a long day with an equally long night. How about meeting at the Tin Cup at nine?"

"Fine with me."

They talked a while longer, but after the long flight the Professor was exhausted. "I think I had better go to the Take 'er Easy and check in. Get some rest. I want to be fresh in the morning."

It was strange, Jud stood thinking as the Professor drove away, this was the first time he could remember him asking for a late start. It was also the first time he hadn't wanted to stay up the night talking about fishing.

After breakfast at the Tin Cup, which was lengthened by the Professor's going behind the grill to share recipes with Sarah as he had done for years, Jud's Willys, driftboat in tow, was following the river toward Elkheart Canyon. The birch groves and cottonwoods along the river were performing card tricks in the autumn sun. The river paralleled the two-lane. Jud was at the wheel. The Professor was in heaven. "What a glorious day it is turning out to be. Look at the light on the trees."

"I'll say. When I got up this morning it was still raining."

The Professor then sat more upright in his seat. "There's a boat down there on the river. Might that be Henry?"

"Very well could be," Jud answered. "His client had him up early and I know they put on the river before eight. If he put in at Bailey's Crossing, he could easily be this far by now. He veered the jeep off the road and pulled a pair of binoculars from beneath the seat. "This could be good.

I think Henry is guiding Mr. and Mrs. Nightmare."

Through the binoculars Jud relayed what he saw. "That's Henry's boat all right"—he hesitated a moment while he focused the glasses—"and in the bow we have the Jimbo who doesn't seem to have missed very many meals. He has what might be best described as a desperate style of fishing. No apparent threat to the fish there. And in the stern, we have Mrs. Jimbo—two hundred pounds no problem. She is—yes, it's confirmed—she's bait fishing. A quick note: the Jimbos are wearing matching lime green jumpsuits. The white fluff bouncing all over the boat would have to be the poodle. And there, in the middle of it all, is our boy Henry at the oars—Henry who has seen better two-day stretches.

"Wait a minute. Jimbo has a fish on. Miracle of miracles. And, judging by the bend of the rod, Henry's frantic rowing, and the velocity of the poodle, it must be a good one. No, check that, he had a fish on. He's lost it." He then handed the Professor the field glasses while trying to control an outburst of laughter, but instead released a chuckle that sounded more like a checkvalve on a steam line. He felt a slight sense of guilt about laughing; here he was, spending a day with the Professor, a prince among men, while his best friend was trapped in a boat with an oil maggot, a hyperkinetic poodle, and a bait-fishing watermelon.

"Yee gawds, what a dreadful-looking scene," said the Professor. "Look at that silly dog. Barking his head off. Oh, yes, I can readily see what you mean . . . she is wretched. Oh my, there he is, Mr. Jimbo; even at this distance—a dreadful man. He seems to be yelling violently. Poor Henry; a horrible day afloat, I judge."

"Well, if Jimbo managed to hook one, then the fishing must be good. Let's get on to the river."

A short while later the *S.S. Lucky Me*, gentle slap of the Elkheart against her bow, was floating downstream, the Professor locked in the knee braces and false casting, Jud pulling at the oars. Letting the line float ahead of him, his fly riding high in the shallows, the Professor turned to

Jud and said, "You know, I've had this old fly rod since 1939. Elizabeth gave it to me."

Jud knew. The Professor had said that or something similar to that many times. He knew about Elizabeth, his wife for thirty years, who passed away the summer that Jud and the Professor met. He knew the rod to be a Winston and how much it meant to him. Elizabeth had bought it for him on a trip to San Francisco during the World's Fair. The old bamboo looked well used and well cared for at the same time. It could stand to be refinished just as well as it could stand another season or two. The Professor, a consummate caster, was a pleasure to watch fish.

For the next hour the fishing was slow, the hour following was even slower. In a lot of ways Jud didn't care if the fishing was slow, for the Professor was a master storyteller with anecdotes from all over the world. They had accumulated enough bad fishing time over the years for Jud to have heard some wonderful tales. But today the Professor was fairly quiet.

"Hey, Professor, you just missed a fish."

"Guess my mind was someplace else. Was he a good one?"

"Naw. Hey, I'm getting hungry. Let's stop and have lunch." Jud rowed ashore at the top of a sharp bend in the river, just after they entered Elkheart Canyon. It was a place where the river flowed straight into a limestone wall and folded over itself; then, boiling and churning, it rolled away, broadening and shallowing into a long green glide. The cliffs towered hundreds of feet above, leaving them a jagged window to the sky.

The Professor was leaning against a large piece of driftwood, and Jud was lying on a path of sand, propped up on one elbow. "Oh, I'm supposed to tell you that Henry's band is playing down at the Tin Cup tonight. He sure would like to see you, but with you leaving tomorrow it may be his only chance."

"Yee gawds. That horrific music. What is the name of Henry's band again?"

"The Mama Juggs Band."

"Oh, the music and the name are so fitting. What a curious blend of a man Henry is—fishing guide, horseshoer, and musician. When I think of all my travels, and the people I have met, Henry would make my list of the most fascinating. But if I am to see him, and I do want to, I seem to have no choice. Tonight—Mama Juggs it is, but only for a short while. I suppose the only harm that could come of it would be to my auditory nerve."

Having had little luck from the boat, they decided to fish the run before them, dividing it so that Jud fished the bottom half and the Professor the top. There were a few fish rising. Jud had yet to set up his rod, and as he did he watched the Professor make his old Winston dance. He cast his line, sending it lit by autumn light, almost gliding through the air, like the silvery strand from a spider's web caught on a breeze.

Pinching a dry fly from his fly box, one of the Red Quills tied from the night before, Jud looked up to see the Professor with his first fish on, his old bamboo jerking and bending against a small rainbow jumping upstream. By the time he had dressed his fly, the Professor had caught a second rainbow—this one fair sized. Two fish in as many minutes is about all the invitation a fisherman can stand, and within moments of their entering the river, Jud had one on as well.

Fishing until they were both satisfied that they had hooked, spooked, or landed every trout in the run, Henry and the Professor started walking back to the *Lucky Me*; on the way they compared their catch. It was like listening in on two men talking out a game of draw poker.

"How'd you do?" Jud anteed.

"I did very well, very well indeed. And yourself?" opened the Professor.

"I did okay. Caught a couple. Lost a real nice one."

"I landed four fish in all, all fairly small, but for the second one—sixteen inches."

"Well, that certainly beats anything I landed. But I wish you could have seen the fish that I lost. If he was an inch he was twenty; had him on for quite a while. Jumped and ran all over the creek. Had him up to the net and he broke me off. He was something. Best fish I've hooked all year."

Poker and fishing are a lot alike. Except in fishing nothing can beat one of a kind. Jud and the Professor had played many such hands together over the years and there could never be a clear-cut winner overall, because, unlike in poker, they released all their fish—they never had to show their cards.

Back in the boat the fishing returned to the morning's slow pace. For long stretches of time the only sounds were that of the old man's Winston fanning the air and the creaking of Jud's oars against their locks.

The silence was broken by the rumblings of the Widowmaker, an ominous name given to an easy rapid. Although Widowmaker Rock, which was roughly the size of a split-level, did sit dead center in the river while two-thirds of the Elkheart roared right into it, and with enough power to reduce the *Lucky Me* into kindling, it was simple to avoid by staying in the third of the river that didn't. If you put your back into it you could miss the rapid entirely, but Jud never liked to do that. He liked to ride the first few waves and then pull into the safer water.

Showing about as much concern as one might entering onto a freeway, Jud readied himself at the oars. He had respect for the Widowmaker even though he could probably row it in his sleep. "Better sit down, Professor. Don't want to lose you." The river was moving faster, the rumble becoming a roar.

The Professor took one more cast, targeting a small pocket of water nearly surrounded in willows. The fly fell short and was quickly swept under.

It snagged and drew his line taut. He tried to jerk it loose, then sat down as instructed.

Doing some last-minute maneuvering, Jud caught a flash of silver in the corner of his eye. He looked to see the Professor's line move out away from the willows. "Hey, Professor, I think your snag is trying to swim upstream."

The rainbow broke water; a very large rainbow; bigger than anything the Professor had hooked in many years, maybe ever. Jud turned to see the fish start its run. Fly line was coiling out of the boat like a harpooner's rope, until it reached the loop pinned under the Professor's foot. He instinctively jumped up, hopping onto one foot, trying to shake the line free from his other. He needed slack or he'd lose his fish.

The first wave of the rapid smashed into the bow, throwing the Professor back over his seat and landing at Jud's feet. He tried righting himself by reaching for the gunwale but accidentally knocked an oar from its lock. The boat turned sideways and the second wave hit it with enough force to twist the freed oar from Jud's hand and it was lost. With no pulling power on one side, they were in trouble. The *Lucky Me* had taken on water. Jud grabbed for the spare oar, which was macraméd in place by fly line.

Other than expletives, nothing was said. They had floated together for years. They both knew exactly what they had to do. Jud had to get the Professor back into his seat, get all that damned fly line off the oar, get the oar back in its lock, and then row his cheeks off if he was going to miss the Widowmaker—if he was going to save his boat.

The Professor knew his part equally well: he was going to get back to his seat, get his fly line away from that damned oar, find his net, and straighten out the slack in his line—if he was going to land that fish.

Rolling out of control, they wallowed through the third wave. They worked feverishly at the oar and by the time Jud had freed it from its lashings, the Professor had unraveled his line from it. Jud slammed it into place and frantically heaved at the oars, spinning their blades like a runaway windmill; but the dory barely moved—half filled with water and sluggish to the oars. No chance of missing the Widowmaker.

The Professor was a man lost in sport; his knees frozen in the braces, both hands holding the rod high above his head as he shouted, "She's still on! I still have her!"

There was little chance the *Lucky Me* would actually smash into the great boulder, the Widowmaker; the force of the water curling back off the rock would cushion that. But there was no doubt they were going over.

"Hold on, Professor! Grab your preserver!" Jud screamed. But in the din of the rapid all the Professor could hear was, "Hold on . . . you deserve her." He thought so as well.

The river hurled the dory directly at the rock, but instead of flipping, it somehow rode the crest of the wave and stalled, almost motionless, at the top of the curl, suspended for a moment between disaster and doom. His oars still whirling, Jud's life flashed before him, while the Professor wondered if he should throw the rainbow a little slack in all this chop.

The boat spun, then slipped stern-first around Widowmaker Rock just as smoothly as a cat takes a corner. Jud tried to ship the oar, but it was too late. He heard the crack of wood. His oar, once a nine-footer, was now a stub.

The river calms quickly after the rapid into a large pool. The *Lucky Me* was all but underwater, yet it was still right side up. The Professor, still somehow standing in the bow, exulted, "That was brilliant! I still have her on!" Jud, just returned from a trip to his Maker, was slow to share in the Professor's enthusiasm. He was glad to see that the lost oar had joined them in the eddy.

The fish jumped, shimmering wet silver. She was a sight; if she'd been a sound, then the sound would have been thunder. The trout jumped close to the boat, shaking her head for freedom and tailwalking her crimson sides. Then she took off on another violent run. Jud looked for the landing net, then for the first time really noticed the condition of their gear: fly boxes, vests, rod tubes, the contents of the cooler—all were bobbing about in the boat. He spotted the net and grabbed it.

The Professor fought the rainbow until the fight had left her. Reeling gently and carefully, he brought the fish to the surface, the trout materializing from the depths like an oncoming ghost. She was spent and easily netted. Lifting the fish from the river, Jud freed the hook, then eased her out of the net to let her recover inside the boat.

"She's tired," Jud said and bent down to help resuscitate the fish. Then he looked up to see that the Professor had gone quite pale. "Are you all right, Professor?"

"A little dizzy perhaps, but I'm fine," he answered, sitting down and watching his trout finning at his feet. "Isn't she a beauty? Quickly put and simply stated, she's the biggest, most beautiful fish I have ever caught in my life. Oh, look at her. Certainly couldn't have done it without your superb rowing."

"But . . ."

"What oarsmanship! The way you kept the boat out in the center, keeping me straight to the fish and away from the willows. The way you went through the rapid backwards was brilliant."

"But Professor, I couldn't . . ."

"If you hadn't pivoted the boat at the exact moment, I would have lost her for certain. She was trying to make it to the other side of the rock, I am sure, but when you started rowing backward, I could really put the butt to her and made her follow us through."

"But the boat was completely out of con——"

"How much do you think she weighs?"

"Six pounds or so," Jud said, deciding to tell him how they really went through the Widowmaker later. Anyway, Jud thought as he moved the trout, cradling it back and forth in his hands to oxygenate the gills, everyone can stand to be a hero for a while.

Everything in the boat seemed to be afloat, and everything, while waterlogged, seemed to be accounted for except . . .

"Oh damn," the Professor swore, when he noticed his camera sinking just past the trout, "I did want to have a picture. This is the kind of trout that will require proof."

The rainbow was showing signs of reclaiming her strength. "Looks like she's ready to go," said Jud, and he handed the Professor the net. "It's your fish—you do the honors."

The Professor scooped the fish up and lifted her overboard, then eased the trout and net into the river. The current played on the netting, and it wasn't but a moment before the great rainbow sensed the opening and swam slowly back into the deep green of the Elkheart.

Bailing for what seemed like most of his life, Jud finally got the *Lucky Me* emptied to the point it would row again. They only had a few bends to go until they reached the takeout. The Professor really hadn't seemed to regain his color. "Listen, are you sure you want to go down to the Tin Cup tonight? It's been a pretty long day and you gotta catch the red-eye tomorrow."

"Nonsense, a trip to Montana without seeing Henry is simply not a trip to Montana. I have given it some thought, and this is how I envision the evening. First, I will return to the motel for some rest, then I will meet you at the Tin Cup for dinner at around eight. Listen to Henry's band for a few selections and be back in my room by ten; that will give seven hours sleep and I can nap on the plane."

At the boat ramp, as Jud bailed the remaining water, the Professor relived the story of his trout once; on the way back to Travers he recounted it twice more; at the Take 'er Easy he dreamed about it; and that evening, over dinner at the cafe, he told it again and again. The fish grew, Jud figured, about a half a pound per telling; and by the time the Professor finished catching it for Junior McCracken, it had grown to well over eight pounds.

"You notice that fish of yours growing any, Professor?" Jud asked as they crossed to the bar side of the Tin Cup where Mama Juggs was getting ready to wind up their first set. They were behind on the Professor's envisioned schedule, but the fish story needed to be told. With each remembrance, the story, like the fish, lengthened; and the Professor grew more animated with every new listener.

"Why, Jud, you know that fish was an easy eight pounds," the Professor said a little sheepishly through a guilty smile.

"I have a new intro to your story when you tell it to Henry."

"Oh, yes? And what is that?"

"Call me Ishmael."

The Tin Cup Bar is a place that somehow drifted away from the continuum somewhere in the late '50s. Inside it was Copenhagen, boots, and Miller Standard Time. The only thing not western was where Sal had his Brooklyn Dodgers memorabilia on display, and even though everything else in the saloon was about as far away as you could get from Brooklyn, the Dodgers, somehow, like Sal himself, strangely seemed to fit—they were, after all, from the right era.

Finally finding a table near the dance floor, they ordered, by tradition, two cognacs from a bottle Sal kept under the bar, a bottle Sal held in reserve only for the Professor. There was no sense in trying to talk above the music. Jud sat back and enjoyed; the Professor observed. Mama Juggs was wound up tight and they were side by side with "Maybelline." The dance floor was crowded and every cowboy with a partner was swinging her. The good-ol'-boy-to-woman ratio was the usual five to one. Everything in a skirt was a queen—at closing time they would be goddesses.

At the break Henry joined them at their table. The Professor stood to shake his hand. "Henry, it's good to see you. How was your day?" he asked, curious to know, and hoping that Henry would then ask how his day had been in return.

"Well, Professor, I guess I'm not too bad for a fella that jest might've had the worst day of his whole life." Sensing that they were in for a story, Jud ordered another round of drinks.

Henry started his day at the beginning. "At seven o'clock I pull up to the Take 'er Easy. There are two fat and ugly people waitin' in front of their room with a poodle and a pile of fishin' gear. All of it brand new. Some of it still in the box. They're ready, trout to tarpon.

"This guy, Jimbo, waddles over to me, smokin' a two-foot cigar and wearin' enough turquoise jewelry to start his own store. He opens the trunk of his Cadillac and there's even more stuff. He tells me to sort through it and pick out what they'll need.

"His wife—are ya ready—'snamed Lulu. And she might have been at one time. Now she's fat. Has thirty pounds on Jimbo. Has pink hair. Talks like Minnie Mouse.

"So, I get 'em all squared away and loaded up and Lulu comes over and hands me this magnum thermos—calls it her libations.

"Just before we git in the truck, Jimbo pulls me over and stuffs a fifty in my shirt pocket and tells me there's another fifty in it if I put him into a lot of fish. Then he says there's another hundred waiting for me if I drown the poodle." Painting an image so ridiculous, Henry had the Professor and Jud howling. He continued on without so much as a hairline crack in his great stone face.

"Well, it didn't take very long, once we were on the river, to figure out that Jimbo and Lulu hate one another. They don't say anything to one another unless it's mean. All day, he hardly catches a fish. She's catching them one after the other, and he's mighty ticked off about it. And every time she'd hook one she'd squeal like a pig, the damned dog would start barking, and all the hairs on Jimbo's neck would stand on end.

"Around noon I was thinkin' about strikin' a deal with Jimbo. I would off the poodle for a hundred and take out Lulu for free. After every fish, she would toss back a few *libations* and say, 'If you wanna catch women, use diamonds. If you wanna catch fish, use a worm.'

"Jimbo hears this too many times. He turns around, half in the bag himself from a flask he's been nippin' at all mornin', and asks me, 'Where did I go wrong? I used diamonds and I caught a fish.'

"Around one o'clock Jimbo's drunk and Lulu's a mess. Jimbo manages to land one, but it's real small. Lulu goes for the jugular, saying, 'That's why daddy don't let you run the company, 'cause you think so small. Just look at your dick.'

"Jimbo goes ballistic, throws down his rod, and starts for her. The poodle bites him; Jimbo knocks the poodle overboard. Lulu goes insane. I fish the dog from out of the drink; it bites me. Then Jimbo picks up his rod and starts fishin' like nothin' has happened, and he turns to me and says, 'You oughta see her naked—make ya gag.'

"Anyway, Lulu has a three-martini lunch. I had one myself, just to calm my nerves. The rest of the day goes along pretty calmly. Lulu passes out and lays on the bottom of the boat all afternoon makin' noises now and then, but nothin' legible.

"So finally we git off the river. Lulu is lights out. Jimbo and I try to lift her into the cab of the truck, but that wasn't gonna git done without a crane and a shoehorn, so we toss her and the poodle in the back. On the way to town, Jimbo hands me a fifty, and wants me to take him and Lulu again tomorrow."

Catching his breath from laughing, the Professor asked, "Are you going?"

"Hey, Jud, that's Peggy's sister over there. Peggy says she's gone through some hellacious divorce, and she's in town on a much-needed vacation. I don't have to remind you about women on much-needed vacations, do I? She is supposed to be real nice and she sure is pretty. I know if I weren't playin' tonight, and Dolores wasn't expecting me, I'd try my damndest to git acquainted."

Purposefully changing the subject, Jud started to tell Henry about the Professor's day. He had him as far as the canyon, on the brink of the big fish, when one of the band members came over with an amp and mike emergency. "I'll have to hear about it on the next break," Henry said, walking away.

"Oh, Henry, I'm afraid I can't stay. I am pretty tuckered out. But, Jud can surely fill you in on the rest of the story, and I shall be back soon to tell you the truth."

"Okay, Professor, I'll see you soon."

Henry once again turned toward the bandstand, when Jud called after him, "Wait a minute. I gotta know if you're taking Jimbo and Lulu fishing tomorrow."

Henry hobbled back to the table, still sore from yesterday's kick. "Well, I tell you guys, I learned something about Henry Albic today. As broke as I am, there ain't enough hunnert-dollar bills to make me go out and do somethin' like that ever again.

"Jud, let's you and me go fishin' tomorrow."

"All right."

"And when you git back, Professor, we'll all go."

"Splendid," he answered while getting up to leave. But when Jud stood up to do the same, the Professor asked, "And just where do you think you are going?"

"Well, it's been a long day for me as well, and I don't mind telling you I'm a little tired."

The Professor put his hand on Jud's shoulder, sitting him back down in his chair. "Listen, here is some advice from an old man to a young man: Ask Peggy's sister to dance. Life is short and it is wiser to dance than to sleep. You can sleep anytime." He sat down again and leaned in close to be heard, as Mama Juggs, feedback solved, was tuning for their next set.

"In 1948 I was living in what is now Zaire, studying and living with the Batwasande. They were typical of Africa's middle tribes. Courtship there was a very tricky business. When a woman comes of age, the tribe will hold a dance and every eligible man in the tribe is there, but the woman will only dance for one man, and he shall be her chosen, her husband-to-be, if he passes a few requirements.

"First, he must show the girl his courage by bringing her the heart of a lion. A lion does not, against a man armed only with a spear, give his heart up easily. Then he, not she, is responsible for the dowry, so showing his true love his good intentions, he must give her family nearly everything he owns—goats primarily. And then, if her family still thinks he is not worthy, they call an end to the engagement, the young man loses all the goats he has given, and the same girl can have another dance and choose another suitor."

"Sounds like California."

"Lucky that we are of this culture and born of this time. For now all a man needs to do is simply tap a lady on the shoulder and ask her to dance; and I use dance metaphorically. It's a chance to meet really, and per chance find that certain someone. I had Elizabeth and in her I had it all."

With that the Professor stood to leave. "You've been a bachelor too long. Join the dance. I'll see you soon." Then remembering, he added, "Oh, is your workshop open? I think I left a pipe up there last night."

"Yeah, it's open."

The Professor patted Jud on the shoulder. "Always good to see you, Jud."

"Good to see you, too, Professor."

Jud sat through another song, staring into his beer and wrestling with the Professor's advice, which he had always regarded as sage. But he hadn't the energy, nor the interest, to dance. He decided it was best just to walk on back to the Boat Works, but as he got up to leave, Peggy Martin's sister appeared next to the table. "It's possible."

"What's possible?" Jud asked, at which point they exchanged quizzical smiles. She tossed a napkin onto his table and written on the back, in the Professor's handwriting: "I would very much like to dance with you. Is that at all possible?"

Extending his arm shyly, he was a bit confused, and not by the Professor's trickery, but by the fact that he was instantly no longer tired. Peggy's sister was pretty; the kind of woman who could give a man a second wind. He stopped short of the dance floor. "There is something I have to know before we dance."

"What's that?" she asked.

"You aren't by any chance Batwasande, are you?"

The next morning Jud was making coffee when Henry arrived. The morning light through the workshop windows lit the sawdust swirls and turned a cedar dory to a near-red.

"Well, you an' Peggy's sister seem to git along right enough last night. Every time I saw you two you were laughing and having a good time."

"Yeah, she's wonderful."

"How wonderful?" Henry asked, leering, as he poured himself a cup.

"I mean, she's a good woman, school teacher, mother; but I don't think she's the one that is going to send me out after the lion's heart or make me give up any of my goats."

"What?"

So, while they went around the Boat Works gathering up what they needed for the day's fishing, Jud explained about the Batwasande. Grabbing his vest, he noticed the Professor's old Winston lying on the workbench, a note pinned beneath it. Jud read the note silently and then, after clearing his throat, read it aloud: "'Jud—What a day it was! I only wish Henry could have been along with us. I feel I must apologize for my long silences this afternoon. This speech I give on Monday has been weighing heavily on my mind. Well, not the speech really, but its content. A retirement speech, I'm afraid. I had no intention whatsoever of retiring—thought of myself as fossilizing right there in Anthro 404.

"'But as it turns out, I have contracted acute leukemia instead. It's a quick and sure-handed killer. Most people live about four months. Old farts like myself can go in a month.

"'Now I have an eternity of some sort to look forward to. I have studied hundreds of religions and while they all have the concept of some kind of God or deity, and some kind of heaven, they rarely agree on where heaven is located and how to get there. The Christians have it somewhere in the clouds. The Buddhists say you have to keep coming back to Earth until you achieve enlightenment— then it's on to Nirvana—wherever that is. While our old friends the Batwasande believe you come back as the ghost of an animal you have slain.

"'I always thought if there is a true and just God, He would allow one to have a say in his or her heaven. A graduate student attended one of my classes several years ago. He was wearing a T-shirt bearing the words: FIRST YOU ARE BORN—THEN YOU DIE. AND WHEN YOU DIE, YOU GO TO MONTANA. Always thought that summed it up quite well.

"'Enjoy the rod; Elizabeth gave it to me, you know. You and Henry have good fishing today. And I'll see you on a river someday.'"

There was nothing they could say. All they could do was feel, and follow the instructions. "Let's go fishing," Jud said. Henry simply nodded.

5

Quintin

EACH SMALL TOWN is allocated one town character. Travers Corners has Quintin. In every town one citizen will be different, ranging from the eccentric and nonconformist to the town drunk or the lunatic-in-residence. But, around Travers, Quintin is regarded only as the local character—for the character he is, and for the character he has.

Having less than anyone in the Elkheart Valley, Quintin still manages to give more than anyone; at least that was what Jud was thinking as he was taking the shortcut from the Tin Cup back to the Boat Works, for up ahead, there was Quintin sweeping up in front of the Roxy just as he did every morning. Jud had just finished one of Sarah's Sunday-morning specials, surely the greatest breakfast in all of Montana, and he was slightly distended from it, but comfortable.

"Morning, Quintin," Jud said.

Quintin smiled, then waved at the Moseley's Ford as it drove past on Main Street. Waving to all passing vehicles was Quintin's self-appointed job. He thought of it as a public service, his civic duty.

"Pretty good crowd last night, Quintin?"

Quintin smiled and nodded.

Motioning to the marquee, Jud asked, "Movie any good this week?"

"Y-y-you bet." But, whether there were three moviegoers, or a packed house, it was a good crowd to Quintin. The film could be a box-office flop or an Academy Award winner—*Ishtar* to *Citizen Kane*—and it was always great cinema through his eyes.

A gust of crisp fall wind shook a few leaves from the maple trees across the street in front of the library, then blew them tumbling, rattling across Main on a five-point scuttle. "Not many leaves left. Winter's in the air," Jud mentioned as he stepped around Quintin's broom. Then he stopped to inspect the coming-attraction posters windowed beneath the marquee. The leaves flew into all the places Quintin had just swept, and the wind, blowing in more work, just made him nod and laugh.

"There are some great sweet rolls down at the Tin Cup, Quintin. Sarah says you better come down and have one."

Quintin nodded.

"Better do it now before you forget."

"Than-th-thanks, Jud, I-I-I'll go right n-n-now," Quintin responded. And although the Tin Cup was no more than a hundred feet from the theater, he took his bike, and managed to wave to three more cars on his short ride.

He is always such a sight, Jud thought as he watched Quintin pedal away. He has two basic outfits that went in and out of fashion according to the weather. In the winter you see Quintin wearing an aviator's cap, a tweed jacket tucked inside of his wool pants, bright orange logger's suspenders, and high-top tennis shoes. His summer ensemble is the same tweed jacket tucked inside his wool pants, and his orange suspenders. But the aviator's cap is replaced by a straw cowboy hat.

If his dress didn't get your attention, his bicycle was bound to catch your eye—not a bike, really, but a three-wheeler with way-oversized baskets, front and rear. A matching pair of small American flags were mounted to the front basket, and fastened along the handlebar was every kind of accessory: three rear-view mirrors, four horns, and two bells with different sounds. Strapped to the rear basket, and waving twelve feet out behind him, was, as always, Quintin's long cane fishing pole.

"Been catching any, Quintin?"

Quintin nodded back as he pedaled away.

Shaking his head, Jud walked on. He had just turned forty-five, and he looked forty-five. But, if you saw him from a distance, his hair mostly gray, wearing glasses, tall, and slightly built, you'd think he was ninety-five. It was his walk. He had a very old walk, though he'd had this same walk since boyhood. On closer inspection, he had the walk of a dreamer, a nomadic rambler out for a stroll. It wasn't a walk, it was more like an amble that had gone adrift.

Ducking down the alley behind the Roxy, he started up a steep path, a shortcut to the Boat Works, with a puzzled look on his face, one that was questioning the unknown.

Most people, especially those who meet Quintin for the first time, come away thinking, "There but for the grace of God go I," and they might easily misread Jud's puzzled expression, mistaking it for pity. But Jud never looked at Quintin from the "grace of God" perspective. He had known Quintin for a long time, and he knew he was looked after and cared for. No, Quintin was Quintin, and that was just the way things happened, Jud reasoned, with or without the grace of God; and he thought about Quintin and his life for the rest of his walk home. . . .

Quintin was a fuzzball in the societal weave, a glitch in the communal strata, a lost ball in the high weeds, both a man and a boy. He was born Quintin Collier in 1939. The son of a trapper, he was raised way up on Birch Creek in what was then the wilderness. Little was known about the Colliers other than they were very seldom in Travers. But it was known they had a boy who was an idiot child. Quintin didn't go to school, never came to town. In 1954, his parents were killed in a car accident, leaving Quintin alone.

He miraculously survived the fatal crash and it was then that Jud and the rest of Travers first saw him. Jud was just eight years old at the time, but he remembered the boy leaving Doc Higgins's office on the morning after the accident as clearly as he remembered meeting him on the street minutes earlier. Little had changed about Quintin since that morning when he first came to town, Jud thought as he entered the back door to his workshop. He'd had the mind of a child then, and now thirty-five years later, he still had the mind of a child.

You notice Quintin's deformities immediately. His spine is twisted slightly, causing one of his shoulders to ride a bit higher than the other and one of his legs to be a little shorter. But, it's Quintin's face that was the tell-all: it portrayed his innocence; it betrayed his manhood; and, as with everything else about Quintin, it was not without a few of its own oddities.

Some faces have a look, some faces have features, some faces have full-length features. Quintin's face is broad and angular, but none of the angles follow the facial norm. His nose is flat, except that it turns up at the end. A boxer's nose. His mouth is twisted and slightly off-center. His cheekbones don't match. His ears are big. His upper lip is always curled back in a smile. He's always smiling.

His eyes are set far apart; one is slightly higher than the other. His left eyelid is sleepy, and beneath it, the eye sort of rolls around. His right eye, in marked contrast—as if his face needed more contrast—holds the startle of constant surprise, wide with the wonder of all that he sees. Jud had always interpreted the astonishment and daydream in Quintin's eyes as the expressions of a curious observer; as though Quintin was not so much looking out as he was looking in; looking in at the marvels, complexities, and insanities of our world; looking in from wherever it is he spent his reality. But wherever it was spent, whether it was a perspective or a place, it was someplace Jud often wished he could visit, for you never saw Quintin without his steady smile and his ongoing amazement.

Balanced between self-reliance and dependency, Quintin walks the fine line of capability. He can take care of himself—to a certain extent. He lives by, cooks for, and looks after himself. But, it's an existence, an order of very simplistic repetitions. In the mornings he sweeps the sidewalks of dust, in the winters he sweeps them of snow. Then, from nine to five, he patrols the streets looking for a door to open for a lady, or for anyone who needs help with a chore: digging a ditch, carrying, lifting, almost anything that doesn't require much in the way of a decision. If no chores can be found, he always has the cars and people to wave to. At five o'clock, during the summer months, he goes fishing every day. At eight he goes home to his shack down by the river, his five or so dogs, and his eight cats. These times are approximations, but he is never off by much more than minutes. Quintin has a schedule, but he doesn't have a watch. Telling time is just a little more math than he can work.

Everyone in Travers looks out for him, especially Mary Hevener, since it's on the edge of the Hevener Ranch, on the banks of the Elkheart, that Quintin lives. Mary checks in on him every morning on her way to town, and he pays her back by helping with the haying or anything else. His reciprocation with the people in town is with corn, for Quintin has a corn patch that's more than an acre, and he delivers his harvest by bicycle to the citizens of Travers every summer. It's the barter system pure and simple between Quintin and the folks in town, as money is something of which he has no understanding. A pittance comes his way every month from the state, but Mary manages it. She gives him pocket change daily, for folding money in his hands brings a new meaning to the term *mad money*.

His concept of money and value can only be matched by his social timing, and usually the three are displayed simultaneously. Like the time he handed out balloons and pocket change at Jim Milton's funeral, or the time he swept up a hundred-dollar bill in front of the Roxy and with it bought and gift-wrapped plumber's friends for all the people at the bank—actions interpreted by the locals as his just trying to cheer people up at a burial, and in the case of the gifts for the bank, well, it was the thought that counts.

There are dozens of other instances when Quintin was off the mark. To a certain degree he can't make it through the day without dropping the ball, losing reality in the lights. No doubt about it, Quintin plays Travers from deep in left field, very deep. But, Jud had a feeling that sometimes Quintin's gifts and deeds were metaphors, for he never knew a larger windbag than the late Jim Milton, and what a miserly old bastard he was. Balloons and loose change were perfect. The symbolism behind the plungers and the bank was only obvious.

Jud opened the door to the wood stove and threw a few more logs on the fire, and had one more thought about Quintin just as the phone began to ring. In a country where the mentally ill were lumped together and abandoned amid the homeless, Quintin had drawn the long straw to be in Travers Corners—a small town that found a place for him. Here he has a home and people who keep an eye on him. If he'd lived in Chicago, he'd have been sleeping on a grate, living in a box. In Travers, he lives fifty yards from his favorite fishing hole. He fishes every day; so while most people would regard Quintin as one of the hapless millions, Jud looked at him as one of the chosen few.

Jud answered the phone, figuring for certain it was Buck Patrelli wanting to know, once again, about the progress of his new driftboat. He'd called every week for the last three months wanting to know when it would be done. Usually, his calls came on Sundays. Jud had a thing about Sundays, especially Sunday mornings; and it wasn't based on anything theological, but sacred all the same. He'd made it clear to Buck not to call on Sunday mornings, and he almost didn't pick up the phone, but this time Jud had the answer he'd been waiting for. "Yeah, Buck. She's ready." *Buck*. Jud found his very name annoying. *Buck—you sort of have to earn a name like Buck. Fifteen years ago he came to Montana, fresh from the streets of Philly, as Freddy Patrelli, and a day later he was Buck Patrelli, Professional Fishing Guide.*

"Hell, that's great news, little buddy. Ya know, it was suppos'ta be ready for me three months ago."

"Well, these boats don't go together overnight, Buck," Jud said, and at the same time thought, *I ain't your buddy, you swaggering, larger-than-everybody-in-life moron. Oh, you may be bigger than I am, but you take away the hot air and bullshit and you'd be nothing but belt buckle and mouth.*

"Now Jud, I've been thinkin' about a coupla things. Because I had to wait an extra three months past the deadline, you had oughta give me some kind of a cut rate."

"Let me remind you again, and quite possibly for the twentieth time, the delays were caused because of all the extra things you kept wanting to add. There was a three-year waiting list on the boat to begin with. And, if you remember, we were nearly two months waiting for your special bobcat-covered seats." *You tasteless creep. You've been thinking about a couple of things. Fat chance. You couldn't think about one thing at a time. If two thoughts were ever to ignite in your Java-like mind, they would cause a fire and heat that I might expect from a pack of wet matches.*

Jud looked over at Buck's boat in the corner of the workshop. It was far from the boat he was known for building: clean, elegant, simple. *I mean if that boat were a car, you'd find it cherry-red, chromed, and cruising the streets of East L.A.*

"Now one other thing I want to talk to you about and that's my professional discount. . . ."

"No, we talked about it, Buck. I don't give discounts."

"Yeah, but Jud, folks are gonna see my deluxe driftboat, man, and they are just gonna wanna have one. Whamo! I give 'em one of your cards. And you got more business than you can handle."

"I got all the business I can handle now." *Anyway, I don't want anybody to know that I had anything to do with your boat. It's an embarrassment to the river. It's the first boat I've ever made that I refuse to put my name on. The only thing missing on that dory is curb feelers, the only driftboat in the world named* La Bamba. *You ignorant . . .*

"Now, I've been a professional guide for seventeen years, Jud, and I am deservin' . . ."

"No discounts, Buck." *Professional discount. You exaggerated stereotype.*

"All right, all right. I'll be over tomorrow mornin' to get her." Click.

Resting the phone back in its cradle, Jud slipped on his work apron and shook his head trying to figure out how in the world someone like Buck could claim professionalism on any level. Jud had trouble with the livelihood of river guide being classified as a profession to begin with. Fly fishing guides could be competent, experienced, accomplished. They could be masters, experts, or veterans, while some of them, like Henry Albie, are regarded as out-and-out wizards. But, they shouldn't be professionals. Doctors, lawyers, and judges were professionals; and there was no way he even remotely wanted to be aligned with that kind of crowd.

Picking up a screwdriver, he headed over to *La Bamba*. He'd told Buck the boat was ready, but there were still a couple of accessories he had to install: the beer holders, swiveling containers especially made from 30.06 cartridges; the bobcat seats. *This boat would float on macho alone, the* S.S. Ricardo Montalban, *Rambo Trout Guide Service*. A wave of nausea hit Jud that one of his boats could ever come to such a fate. *What have I done?*

Monday morning, as Jud headed in for coffee at the Tin Cup, he looked up the street and waved to Quintin who was sweeping up at the Roxy. Today was going to be different from yesterday. It was much warmer and it was sure to turn into an Indian summer afternoon, maybe the last one of the year—the last autumnal offering. It was bound to be a great day despite the fact that Buck would be by for the dory.

All was in place at the Tin Cup. Sarah was at the grill and Henry was at his stool.

"Morning, Henry," Jud said and waved at Sarah, who could only roll her eyes in the heat and the frenzy of short-ordering to a packed cafe. Doris hustled past. She was picking up orders, she was filling out bills, running for syrup, running for catsup. She was earning her tips. Grabbing a couple of omelettes, she asked, "Hey, Jud. Do me a favor, will ya? Grab your own coffee? I'm kind of runnin' behind."

"Sure." He walked behind the counter, grabbed the coffee pot, and looked around a restaurant filled with caps and hats. He filled his cup and he warmed Henry's. "What's with all the ranchers in town?"

"Big bull sale at the fairgrounds."

"Oh, that's right. It's today. I forgot."

"What's goin' on with you?" Henry asked as Jud poured a cup for Bill McHale, who was sitting down next to Henry.

"I've got Buck coming over to pick up his boat this morning," he answered, setting the pot back on its burner and returning to his seat at the counter. He nodded toward Bill. "Morning, Bill."

"Mornin', Jud. Mornin', Henry," the old rancher greeted, then shook the newspaper open and started checking the day's stock reports. Bill looked like he just stepped from the feed lot, and smelled a little that way as well; drove a beat up old pickup; and was worth millions. He'd be a player at today's sale.

Henry turned back to Jud, then saw Buck coming through the front door. "Looks like yer day is about to begin."

Spotting Jud at the counter, Buck made his way to the rear of the Tin Cup. He puffed himself up for his entrance and strutted through the cafe in his usual getup. He was giant black hat, rattlesnake hatband; he was silk kerchief, tied just so; he was leather vest, turquoise on most of his fingers, and an elkhorn belt buckle. A bear tooth hung around his neck by a gold chain you could tow a car with. His tight-fitting jeans were tucked into a pair of python boots. Buck was a walking parody of himself, straight from central casting. He equated his own appearances as something akin to John Wayne's dropping by, a treat for the little people. The ranchers looked up to see only another joke from out of town.

"You should have to pass some kind of a test to move into this state," Henry said under his breath, but it was loud enough to make Jud laugh, and make Bill look up from his paper and laugh with him.

Then Buck was upon them. "Hey, little buddy. My boat ready?"

"Yeah," Jud said, then slowly took a sip from his coffee.

"Well, let's go up and git 'er. Ya made me wait for three and a half months. You're not gonna make me wait while you have breakfast now, are ya?"

Jud looked off with a face that said he would give it some thought.

"I got clients out there waitin'. A couple of big shots. I'm gonna float 'em from Stone Creek to Town Bridge. I love this weather. Don't you? Fill yer lungs, makes you wanna howl at the moon."

"Every time," droned Jud. *Precious little doubt that any of that crisp mountain air will make it north of your neck. I can't stand to listen to this guy talk—a Southside Philly accent trying to emulate a Rocky Mountain drawl. It's like Sylvester Stallone imitating Slim Pickens.*

Standing, Jud then headed for the door. Nothing had been said between Henry and Buck. They didn't like each other and hadn't for a long time, going back to a time fifteen years before when Henry caught Buck and two clients with three times their legal limits. Henry's discourse on catch and release elevated that day from yelling to breaking Freddy from Philly's nose.

Shortly after Buck and Jud had left, Quintin came into the cafe. He was looking for Jud, but couldn't see him, and left without waving to anyone. He headed for the Boat Works. He had big news.

By the time Quintin bicycled up the hill to the Boat Works, the boat had been loaded, and Buck was walking back to the workshop with Jud to take care of the bill. "I find it mighty hard to understand why you can't give a professional discount, I mean I . . ."

"J-J-Jud!"

Halfway through the door Jud looked back to see Quintin, who was pedaling hard. "J-J-Jud!" Quintin called out again. Jud stopped and stepped back outside.

Breathing hard from coming up the hill, his exciting news, and the fact that Buck was there made Quintin's stammer more pronounced. Quintin didn't like Buck. He made him nervous.

"Y-Ya wanna kn-n-ow what I s-s-s-saw, J-Jud—Jud?"

"Yeah. What did you see, Quintin?"

"W-w-w-well. Ya kn-n-now down b-b-b-by the i-i-i-island?"

"Yeah," Jud answered.

"I s-s-saw a b-b-big one, a re-really b-b-big one," and Quintin spread his hands three feet apart.

Quintin might live on the outskirts of reality, Jud thought, but he also knew that Quintin never lied. He just had trouble understanding weights and measures, inches and feet; of course, this was an affliction shared by all the global fraternity of anglers. But, while Jud knew, as would anyone who fishes for trout, that Quintin's estimation of the fish he saw was greatly exaggerated, he also knew that Quintin had seen a really big fish.

"W-w-w-ould you m-m-make m-me a fly?"

"Sure I will."

Buck looked over to his truck and to a pair of pacing clients, "the big shots," who were looking at their watches. "Hey, this is touchin', you helpin' the village idiot, Jud, but I got clients waitin'."

"Can you come back a little later, Quintin?" Jud asked.

"O-o-o-okay." And Quintin was on his bicycle and gone.

Jud had added up Buck's bill yesterday, a very detailed bill of hours spent on Buck's dory. Then once again, when the bill was presented, Buck tried for a discount; and again Jud stood firm. He would never give this guy a discount, and after the "village idiot" crack he wanted to tack on another hundred. He was silently furious and in his mind, instead of the verbal barbs that usually formulate whenever Buck was involved, he saw himself instead, just for a few seconds, as George Foreman, and Buck upside down and bleeding in the corner.

Buck grabbed his new oars leaning in the corner of the workshop. They were twelve-footers, roughly four feet longer than any oar on the river, and ten pounds heavier than common sense dictates, but the long oars were just another way for Buck to stretch his image, just part of the carney. The bigger the oars, the bigger the man.

"Just curious, Buck, what are you going to name her?" Jud stood there with the knowing gloat of a man who had just negotiated the better end of a deal. It was a look he controlled, and he was enjoying its effects on Buck. Quite an effective weapon, the smirk.

"*Charlene*," Buck snapped and threw his oars in the back of the truck. He told his clients to get in. "Thanks for my professional discount there, little buddy."

"Anytime." *You simple son-of-a-bitch*. Then, Jud laughed, thinking *Charlene* was perfect. Buck had named his boat after his wife. Charlene was the woman you'd see sitting at the poker machines, smoking extra-longs and drinking ditches. She was the woman from K-Mart, the roller-in-the-hair nightmare haunting the mall. Charlene was an unrefined mess of woman. But, as wretched as she was, when she decided to really get dressed up, put her wig-hat on her head, and fire up the mojo, she could be absolutely disgusting. She was all glitz and low-cut. She was sleaze. She was ghastly, but she had money.

Buck's pickup was a match for his boat, outfitted with every accessory known to Detroit. It had so many running lights that at night it looked like an oncoming town. As he drove down the hill, he was telling his clients how Jud had given him a great price on the boat, because Jud knew it would be good for his business to have Buck be seen rowing one of his dories. The deal called for a drink, and they passed the whiskey around once more. It wasn't their first time at the flask this morning, but this round wasn't just a good ol' boy's social—Buck needed a drink. He had told Charlene he would be getting the dory for roughly half of what he had just paid for it. His spending always put her on the fight. She would be a raving, screaming bitch about this one.

At the bottom of the drive waited Quintin. He brought about as much practical application to his sense of time as he did to the concepts of weights and measures. So, when Jud asked him to come back later—well, on Quintin's clock, *later* had a lot of latitude. In his world *later* could waver anywhere from the next moment to sometime next year. His approach to this *later* was just to wait for Buck to leave. He didn't like Buck.

When the pickup and trailer rumbled down the drive he could see Buck and his dudes. They rolled by and the big shots stared at him. He heard Buck's voice; then came the laughter. The laughter Quintin had hated for a lifetime. The laughter that ran away, the laughter that slithered over turned shoulders, the laughter that came when strangers passed. The murmured sting. The whispered knife. The laughter of ridicule. The laughter that brought a searing pain to his heart and mind. Quintin had learned as a boy never to look back at the laughter; it was always the same: faces turning away, darting eyes, glances, sniggers suppressed by mean smiles. It hurt most when the laughter came from children.

He did look up to take one more look at the boat; he loved that boat more than any he had seen Jud build before. It had so many things hanging from it.

Then it was back up the hill. Jud was a little surprised to see Quintin back so quickly, but then Quintin was full of surprises; like the time he dressed his dogs up in Christmas lights, brought them to town, and plugged them in.

So, the morning passed. Jud tied up a few flies. Quintin swept out the workshop in trade. Jud then went down to the bank with Buck's check to cash, as Buck's checks were known for their bounce. Travers was alive. The grandstand at the fairgrounds was almost filled with ranchers.

Later in the day Henry stopped by the Boat Works and talked Jud into going over to the fairgrounds. Jud had little interest in going to a bull sale, but then Henry reminded him that Sarah was cooking for the auction and she promised Henry she would save them some beef and a little of her chili.

Winter was just a page away on the calendar, and surely this would be one of the final days of a warming sun. It was also wonderful that it happened to land on a Monday. He would have liked to go fishing himself, because Jud had a thing about fishing on Mondays; it gave him the same ethereal feeling as playing hooky.

Out on the river, Buck and the big shots were about to finish their float trip. It was a short day, since one of the big shots, known to his friends as Sid "the Shiv" Morelli, needed to be on the move; a Senate Committee wished to talk to him. The other, Benny "Fingers" Bandalucci, was going to stick around for a few more days. Montana was a good place to lay low, since Morley Safer was wanting to ask him some questions. This all supported the birds-of-a-feather theory Jud and Henry subscribed to: certain clients migrate to certain guides. In Buck's case, the clients sort of oozed in his direction. They were usually scum, and he being slime, the client-guide relationship was almost symbiotic, like algae and fungus.

The afternoon had gone poorly for Buck. The booze had hit him the wrong way. His gut twisted, but that wasn't from the whiskey, it was from nerves. Seeing Charlene was only a couple of hours away, and the inevitable war would be on over money. The whiskey bottle was empty. The fishing had been slow and Sid was complaining steadily. Buck pointed to the cooler with two very large rainbows dead on the ice, but this wasn't enough for Benny and Sid, who began reminding him of the thirty-trout-day promised them. No doubt about it, fishing was slow. They wouldn't have the two in the cooler if Buck hadn't rigged them up with worms through the no-kill section.

Quintin was already at home getting ready to go fishing. He had adjusted his sweeping and waving schedule to his fishing day by starting everything earlier, since the afternoons were getting shorter.

Now, it goes without writing, that Quintin has his own style when it comes to the art of the angle. He fishes with a long cane pole; this was logical, since the handling of line, the reeling of reels, the timing of the cast were just too much hand–eye coordination at once. He could handle his three-wheeler, a broom, or a shovel, and a hoe for his corn, but his motor skills stopped there. The cane pole was a natural.

But it wasn't his tackle that made his approach to fishing so unique; it was his method. Years ago he had seen a movie at the Roxy. Jeff Chandler was leading the Marines and he had leaves and branches coming out of his helmet and pack; camouflage; surprise attack. So, Quintin would prepare himself for his pastime by sticking willow branches under his suspenders, twigs up his sleeves, down his neck, in his coat, and down his pants. He darkened his face with mud. Then, with stealth, his system was to sneak in above his trout, slowly lift his cane pole over the river, and let the current swing his line, then his fly—the one Jud had tied for him—to the trout below him.

The Elkheart River flows into Travers Corners on a big S-turn. Quintin was fishing in the middle of the S, the fairgrounds were at the bottom of the S, and Buck was about a half a mile above Quintin and floating into the S. "S": the first letter of S.O.S., the first letter in shipwreck, and the first letter of what was about to hit the fan.

Coincidence, fate, and circumstance, the forces that play on everything: people, places, inanimate objects, everything. Even the mighty cottonwood is subject to a destiny. But, when coincidence, circumstance, and fate braid, the crossroads become happenstance, and the timing becomes karma. Karma can come in an instant, it can come in a lifetime, it can come in a thousand years.

Jud's outlook on karma was as follows: If Einstein had a grasp on the relative, and theoretical time does travel in circles, then one should think of karma not in terms of providence, but as a ride.

Creeping along the riverbank, moving as he thought a willow bush might move, his camouflage slightly betrayed by his bright orange suspenders, Quintin neared the place where he had seen the big trout. Just as he was about to drop his fly on the water, there came a sound like rolling thunder, followed by cracks like rifle fire, then more thunder, and it kept rumbling. The sound echoed upstream and it came from the channels. He scrambled up the bank for a better view. From there he could see that the dead cottonwood on the top of the island had fallen into the river and in its fall had taken several other old trees with it. Branches, trunks, and deadfall were being pinned in the rocks and the swift current. The left and only navigable channel was blocked.

Knowing this was the kind of thing he should tell someone, but not exactly clear as to why, Quintin headed for home and his bicycle. But as soon as he turned to run, he heard voices. He looked up to see Buck and the big shots upstream and floating for the left channel.

This was the part of the float Buck had been looking forward to all day, the chance to see how *Charlene* would handle in the rock garden and tumbling currents of the left channel. He would waltz her pretty as you please with his big oars through the boulders, then it was just a couple of hundred yards to Town Bridge and the takeout at the fairgrounds. But five tons of cottonwood and some very heavy karma dammed their way.

"St-st-stop!" Quintin shouted with his arms waving.

Buck, despite the fact that he had just floated past him, hadn't seen Quintin, but then he looked more like part of the underbrush than anything else. Then Buck spotted him and Quintin heard Buck's voice, followed by the laughter of all three, the mean-spirited laughter that always made him turn away. He neither shouted nor waved again, but just looked on as Buck began to pick up speed and veered away as he headed down the left channel.

"Hey, dat's da little weird guy from dis morning. He looks like he's trying t' warn ya about sumpin'," said Benny.

"Da guy's dressed up like a bush, and he looks serious to ya," laughed Sid the Shiv.

"Quintin's nuttier than a fruitcake. He's always waving his arms. Waves to every truck and car what comes into town. Waves to everybody. Don't mean nothin'. The village idiot," Buck explained, still laughing. "Last winter he was seen ridin' his bike down Main Street in nothin' but his long johns. And he was carrying bags and bags of frozen corn." What Buck didn't tell Sid and Benny was that Quintin was only reacting to something he had overheard—that the Johnsons were having hard times and didn't have much in the way of food or clothing. So he gave them what he had.

They were all laughing hard. Quintin heard them until their laughter was lost to the river's roar, then he ran back to his vantage point on the knoll. Something, either very good or very bad, was about to happen, but he just wasn't sure. Maybe he should have waved harder. He didn't like Buck. The boat would be fine because they float.

Puffed up over the oars, Buck began to dance *Charlene* through the rapids, impressed with himself, his boat, his rowing, and his long oars. "Boy, this boat handles sweet," he shouted to the clients, then let out a rodeo yell.

Buck had another hundred yards left on his ego. Karma was about to cut in. The gods knew it, Quintin knew it, Buck and the big shots didn't have a clue.

The fallen cottonwood came into view. Buck began shouting and pulling on the oars. In a word, Buck panicked. He tried desperately to pull the driftboat to the shore. But the oars were too long for a tight situation, and they bounced off the exposed rocks instead of catching any water. *Charlene* slid up on a boulder that was only partly out of the water. She spun and hit another rock. Her bow caught again in the current and she turned free only to spin and pinball into a boulder about half her size. She hit hard. The jar knocked Buck and Sid from their seats. Benny was thrown from the boat.

In seconds, *Charlene* was over to the cottonwood. Her turned-up bow rode up on the branches. The power of the river pinned the boat into the tree and held her there. Water surged all around. Benny was swept into a mangle of broken limbs, then disappeared beneath the tree.

Buck and Sid scrambled around the boat, crying out the possibilities that might save their lives. *Charlene* shifted as the two men, Buck crawling over Sid, climbed out onto the trunk. The limbs beneath her cracked, then gave way. *Charlene* started to ship water.

The current twisted the driftboat again, then rolled her lengthwise against the cottonwood. The river filled her instantly. Buck was white and frozen with fear. Sid was terrified—shock had set in. A tree, taken into the river by the cottonwood's fall, broke loose upstream and was floating like a battering ram toward *Charlene*, her captain, and half the crew.

Quintin looked on, knowing that somehow the oncoming tree was going to change things. He'd watch and see, then run down and find out what Buck was doing.

The snapping and crackling sounds of cured and finished wood carried as far upstream as Quintin, but over at the fairgrounds, neither the violent fall of the giant cottonwood on the island nor the crunching of a day-old driftboat could be heard above the clamor of bulls, cattle trucks, and auctioneers.

On the top row of the grandstands sat Jud, Henry, and Sarah, warm from the afternoon sun, the glow from a couple of beers, and Sarah's chili. A shout was heard, then more shouts, then people running to see. Cowboys and hats were standing like a stadium wave, with all faces turning toward the river; people were pointing and yelling.

From the bleachers, Jud, along with Sarah and Henry, stood to see what was causing all the stir. There, in the middle of the river, was a man struggling to stay afloat by holding onto a limb. A couple of ranch hands dove into the river with ropes and lashed onto the man. The call came back up the hill for someone to get Doc Higgins.

Slowly moving down the trunk, working their way through the branches, Buck and Sid looked back as the tree hit. *Charlene* was crushed. The added weight of the tree moved the cottonwood and it rolled another ten feet only to get wedged again. The roll shook Buck loose and he was thrown into the current.

By the time Quintin had made it down to the scene, Buck had just been swept around the bend, and the cottonwood had broken free once again and then lodged in the shallows. And even though Sid could have just slid from the trunk into one foot of water, two feet from the shore, he was frozen to the tree. Only after much prodding and pulling did Quintin convince Sid it was safe to step onto the bank.

It was a short walk to the fairgrounds and Sid was reluctant to follow Quintin, after what he had been told about him by Buck. Sid had nearly lost his life. He was bruised and cut, and Quintin just smiled his normal smile. Sid then could hear the sound of people and traffic and see the flags above the grandstand. He allowed Quintin to help him, remembering it was Quintin who had tried to warn them about the danger.

Quintin helped Sid across the nearly dry right channel and up the embankment. They were spotted, and men ran down to help Quintin, who was struggling under the weight of a fat and hypothermic Sid.

When Buck cleared the island and floated into view, Henry and Jud left the stands for a closer look. Thinking a grandstand was the best place to watch such a fiasco, Sarah stayed behind. By this point many of the ranchers were filtering out of the stands, as were the camera and crew of KMTN out of Missoula who were there covering the sale. Charlene, faking concern for her man, was also on her way out of the bleachers and heading down to the river. She was in high heels and tight-fitting pants, and she'd been drinking gin. Charlene was extra-mean on gin.

"What happened?" asked the first ranch hand to get to Buck.

Buck was trying to catch his breath and summon up his bravado as he realized that his wreck had been seen by nearly every rancher up and down the Elkheart. "A big cottonwood on the island gave way. We didn't have a chance," Buck answered, battered but not bleeding. He attempted the posture of a man who had just laughed in death's face. But his bravado and posturing lost something against his pallor and trembling. It was an explanation anybody who had floated the left channel could appreciate: a narrow channel, a giant cottonwood, fast water on a blind bend.

Weaving through the crowd came Quintin, and when he reached Jud and Henry, he started to explain. " I t-t-tried t-to t-tell them. I w-w-aved a-a-and I yelled. But he," pointing at Buck, "d-d-didn't stop."

Charlene had made her way through the crowd, attracting attention to herself by feigning concern for her man. Henry saw her coming and purposely timed his comment as she wiggled past. "Damn. A five-thousand-dollar driftboat this mornin' and nothin' but kindling by afternoon."

Jud saw it all register in Charlene's gin-coated stare as she looked to the river and saw nothing but flotsam and the wreckage of her namesake. She flew into a rage. "You stupid son-of-a-bitch." She was all cocked and ready to slug Buck, when she noticed that the KXLA camera was on her. Charlene has a thing about cameras; her breasts and lips inflate whenever one is pointed at her. But the camera was off her quickly as Sid was being helped on his way to Doc Higgins, who was already treating Benny at the fairgrounds office. Sid saw Quintin trying, once again, to explain to Jud and Henry what had happened. "Dat's da little guy," Sid pointed. "He tried to warn us, but da Buck here jest kept on goin'. Ya dumb . . ." Sid then noticed the crew from KMTN and his instant reaction was to hide his face from the camera. Then he moved toward Buck: "I'll git you for dis." Those are words not to be taken lightly when they come from someone whose nickname is Shiv.

The debris and cargo, from the once and garish *Charlene*, floated in the eddy below the bridge and kids from town were salvaging the wreckage as it circled into the shore. A cooler came floating in. The Wilson kid undid the straps, opened it, and held up the two large rainbows. Taking fish in the no-kill section was the same offense Henry had pasted Buck for fifteen years ago, but he was too old for that sort of thing now. This time he needed to do something that would have a lasting effect. "Hey, cameraman," Henry called over to the KMTN crew, "swing yer camera down on the kid by the river holdin' those trout. Rainbow trout are protected here. Those fish were taken from a no-kill section. And the outfitter's name, who was slimy enough to do this, is Buck Patrelli. That's all I got to say."

Buck was crazy with embarrassment.

Shouting over her shoulder, Charlene stormed her way back through the crowd. "I am gonna kick yer sorry ass when you git home." In addition to everything else, Buck was now being laughed at. Buck started walking fast toward his pickup and his now-useless boat trailer.

Quintin felt bad about the boat, he admired it so. It had more things hanging on it than his bike. He didn't like Buck, but he loved that boat.

Quintin approached Buck to tell him he was sorry. He wasn't sorry about him being thrown in the river. He wasn't sorry about the entire town laughing at him. He was just sorry about the boat. He came up to Buck, with his ever-present smile, "S-s-sorry . . ."

Something within Buck snapped. He wanted to lash out at something or someone, and Quintin, the symbol of all his misery, was in his way and grinning. He slapped Quintin to the ground. "Ya goddamned moron."

Henry, who was on the ragged edge anyway about the trout, forgot, for a heartbeat, that he was too old. It was a picture-perfect right cross, vigilante justice—one step up for Henry, two steps back for Buck, where he fell into a heap, upside down and bleeding.

Quintin ran through the crowd, laughing. He felt so much joy. He loved seeing Buck upside down and bleeding, and when Quintin felt this happy there was only one thing to do, and that was to go home and ride his bike, toot its horns and ring its bells, until he got all his dogs howling. Then he'd do a little fishing.

The live-action team from KXLA did a great job of editing and turned the whole incident into a hilarious story. The video caught a feed out of Missoula—it had missed the nightly news, but was syndicated all over the Rockies by eleven o'clock. None of this, of course, escaped the FBI or Morley Safer; both were in Travers before daylight. Travers Corners, where nothing ever happens locally, was suddenly in the news nationwide: Benny Bandalucci, a known mobster, was taken by the FBI. First thing Monday morning, Morley Safer was at Doc Higgins' clinic, where Sid had been ordered to spend the night because of his dangerously elevated blood pressure.

Of course, the cornering of a famous underworld figure brought the incident to the front page, and the following night Dan Rather closed the news with the story.

CBS aired it all, from the wreckage of the *S.S. Charlene*, to the threat from Sid the Shiv, and Henry's right cross. Every eye in the Elkheart was on Rather that night as he closed. "It seems that this story didn't end there," he reported, trying to keep a straight face. "Because of this broadcast's being aired by KIFX, our affiliate in Philadelphia, the outfitter Buck Patrelli was hit today with fifteen years' worth of back alimony and child-support payments. Also, today his current wife sued him for divorce, a hefty fine was imposed by the Department of Fish and Game, and his license to outfit was suspended by the Montana State Board of Outfitters. Oh, and his boat, which was completely destroyed in the accident, was not even one day old. I guess, for a fishing guide, these kinds of days would come under the heading of 'Bad Carpma.' And that's part of our world tonight. Good night from CBS." He then began laughing with the studio crew as the highlights from the fairgrounds showed again while the credits rolled.

Jud turned off the television smiling and shaking his head and then headed for the kitchen to see what he could do about supper. His refrigerator was looking very bachelorlike: duplications of every known condiment, but an entree was going to be a problem. From the kitchen window, pedaling out of the dusk, he could see the silhouette of Quintin coming up the drive.

When he saw Jud lit in the kitchen window, Quintin merely raised his arms and spread his hands as far as his reach would let him. Jud flashed a thumbs up, and Quintin was gone, back into the fading light.

A big fish for Quintin. Jud laughed out loud, looking at the improbable outline of Quintin and bike, at the boy in a man's clothes. More karma.

Karma was the mainstay of Jud's beliefs; something in and of itself he sometimes found to be a worry—hanging his philosophy on something as ephemeral as karma. It seemed so shallow and wistful when you compared it to the beliefs of Fundamental Baptists. But karma is taken lightly in America, where it has become a colloquialism for: You get what you deserve. What goes around comes around. You reap what you sow. Nothing religious. Nothing serious. If a man brags then fails, it's karma. If a priest wins the lottery, it's karma.

The rest of the world thinks of karma as the power formed when coincidence and mysticism collide in a flashpoint of equity. But to a Buddhist, Karma is the whole deal, the path to your next existence. Jud, whose own religious vent swung freely from atheism to pantheism, revered karma as a mixture of whimsy, chance, eastern religions, all the misunderstood energies of the universe, and the unknown. A weighty group of variables.

The Hindus think you carry around your own personal karma. Jud looked on karma as a free agent, something that was always on the move. Opening a can of soup, he wondered how karma might travel; did it ride on some strange elliptical light, or did it bounce like radio waves—station KRMA? Maybe it didn't move at all; maybe karma just holds its ground and waits for you. Jud favored the "blind pig at the wheel of a bumper car" theory: that karma is indiscriminate, eventually slamming into everyone.

Maybe karma just falls to earth, he reasoned, as he reached for a box of crackers. But, however karma travels, and Jud felt this in his heart to be true, when it catches up with you—justice will be served.

Karma had been just and very thorough in Travers Corners the last two days. Jud smiled as he stirred his dinner and looked out the window into the night. Buck left town for Philly on the bus, hoping to blend into anonymity: the karma he deserved. While Quintin caught a very large trout: the karma he had deserved.

What Jud didn't know was that the brown trout Quintin had caught that day, if measured and weighed, would have been recorded at thirty-one and one-half inches long; seventeen pounds, seven ounces. But weights and measurements were of no interest to Quintin. Most anglers would have taken such a fish home, a trophy for the den, knowing that such a trout doesn't come to an angler more than once in a lifetime, or a thousand lifetimes. But Quintin, dressed as shrubbery, aviator cap on, fishing his long cane pole, wrestled with that giant brown trout for almost an hour, only to admire it and let it go.

Quintin certainly qualified as different, but he wasn't crazy.

6

~

Three Yahoos

THE CARRIE CREEK sign creaked in the evening breeze and cottonwood blooms spiraled halfway up its posts, then spun free on the wind to scurry and drift into the corners and the doorways of the Boat Works. The sign read CARRIE CREEK BOAT WORKS AND GUIDE SERVICE and the words would have been lost to the night had it not been for the light shining down from the upstairs window. Jud's shadow moved along the walls and ceiling and grew larger as he walked to the bookcase.

He stood browsing for some time, hoping that some title, either previously, partially, or never read would leap out at him. Then he looked to the top shelf thinking that things forgotten seem to march their way to oblivion in some kind of universal order. Old photos seem to find their way to the back of the closet, old music slowly sorts itself to the rear of the stack, and old books make the climb to the top shelf to gather dust and respectability.

The summer wind parted the curtains and filled the room with that rarified and seldom-felt warmth that loosens you and sends you tumbling through the memories born on such nights, those top-down and whistling, rocking in baby's arms, halcyon nights. Romance and laughter sail on such a wind. It sets the dreamer to dreaming. It blows the reader to the top shelf.

On tiptoe, Jud fingered the spines of the books from the uppermost reaches of the bookcase. He was looking for something light. He was looking for something funny, but most of all, he was looking for something short, since he'd been at the oars ten hours today, rowing against an upstream wind and a slow day of fishing.

"Ah, just the ticket," he said aloud to an empty room. He pulled down an anthology of Mark Twain; a holdover, as most of the books on the top shelf were, from college.

Brushing away a cobweb, he began leafing through the pages, until the pages bucked and the book skipped open to a thirty-year-old bookmark, an old photograph. He stepped closer to the lamp on his desk. As he held the old photograph under the light, a smile spread across his face, the smile that comes from finding something long believed to be lost.

There they were in black and white—now almost thirty years ago, in 1964, their eighteenth summer—standing in the middle of Walker's field; stripped to the waist; hay hooks dangling from their hands and posing for Old Man Walker's camera.

There was Henry on the right, short and muscular with a crew cut, looking very much the football hero; on the left was himself, the poster boy for the gangling teenager; and towering above them both, there was Donny in the center, but then he always was. Jud remembered that moment as if it had been only an hour ago and the summer of '64 as if it had ended yesterday. He settled back into his easy chair and stared into the photograph until the young men, boys really, in Walker's hayfield and the Elkheart Valley blended into just what they were—one.

It doesn't take long to go back to where you've been. . . .

"Now how am I gonna git a good picture with you yahoos a-hoppin' around like three farts in a skillet. Now stand still or you'll blur fer certain."

"Well, Mr. Walker, blurrin' would be the kindest thing you could do for a face like Henry's," Donny quipped.

This prompted Henry to box thin air. "Right after we're done hayin' I am gonna make you even uglier."

Finally, Jeff Walker settled them back into the viewfinder and the picture was taken. "That about does it for this year, boys. A few more bales and you'll be through. When ya git 'er done, come on up to the house and the missus will write out yer pay. Ya did a good job."

All three boys said their thanks and started walking back to the tractor and bale wagon. But as soon as Old Man Walker was out of earshot, Henry turned and began to half-circle around Donny with his hands raised. "Jud, did ya hear how this dipshit talked to me, and in front of Old Man Walker?"

Donny laughed. "Jeez, Henry, Old Man Walker already knows who the dipshit around here is. Wasn't it you he watched run his baler into the ditch yesterday?"

"Well, I think I jest might have to slap some respect into that pitiful face of yours," and Henry threw two quick slaps, one of them connecting.

Donny made a grab for Henry, his arm reaching out like a hinged timber, but Henry was too quick. "Okay, peckerhead," Henry said in his most menacing voice, "you've been asking for it all afternoon and now you are going to git it."

"I'd be careful, Donny. Henry here is the meanest thing on this ranch, 'cepting, of course, Old Lady Walker," Jud interrupted.

Laughing, Donny let down his guard and Henry struck. They slapped one another as hard and as fast as they could swing. Their boots pounded up the dust and the hay chaff swirled. Jud made his usual contribution to their fight by remaining on the sidelines. Being the slightest of the three, he knew that interference meant participation and that participation meant pain. He knew, and had known since they were small, that his best armament against the two was his humor.

Jud had watched these two go toe-to-toe since they were able to stand.

The end result was always the same: Donny systematically dismantled Henry. He looked on but was paying little attention. He had other things—important things—on his mind. He leaned against the tractor's tire and thought about the night ahead and Jeanne. . . .

The phone rang and jangled him back from somewhere deep in 1964. "Hello . . . Hi ya, Henry . . . Sure, you can borrow it . . . I won't need it back until next week . . . Hey, you won't believe what I just found stashed away in a book . . . No . . . No . . . You'd never guess . . . I'll bring it down to the Tin Cup tomorrow, and I'll bring the belt sander, too . . . Okay . . . Right . . . See ya."

Easing down under the covers, Jud had one more look at the old photograph; God, how young they were! He switched off the light. The room was dark but the images were as bright as the July sun that lit that old black-and-white. . . .

"Hey, you guys," Henry said, picking gravel from his forehead and winded from the bout, "Dolores's cousin is in town. I say we buy a jar of the Crogans, take Jeanne, Dolores, and the cousin up to Frenchman's Meadows, git 'em a little loose on whiskey, and then show 'em the stars." The color was slowly returning to his face. Donny had just administered his Chinese-puzzle hold on Henry for about the thousandth time, and Henry said this while trying to snap his anatomy back into place.

"Show 'em the stars" was the trio's euphemism for taking their girlfriends to the hills and making out. Joe Crogan's moonshine was always the needed catalyst.

"That sounds good to me," Donny said eagerly. "I'll take Dolores and you can take her cousin."

"Why would Dolores have anything to do with a dipstick like you?" Henry quipped, prompting a few more slaps between the two of them.

"What do ya say, Jud?" Donny asked. "We could go down to Miller's Bridge and do a little fishin'. We could have the girls meet us down there around eight-thirty. We'll barbecue some steaks, have a few rounds of the Crogans, and head to the Meadows. Full moon tonight." Henry gave a short howl.

But Jud's night was all planned, and it didn't include Donny or Henry. He had thought of *this* night, nightly, and sometimes all night for a week. For last Saturday night he and Jeanne had come real close; closer by far than ever before; almost all the way, but then he had his weekly run-in with the Pope. Catholic girls. "Naw, Jeanne and I are going to the movies."

Tonight he had his mom's car, which had a great radio and a large back-seat. He would have a jar of the Crogans, and a cooler with ice and coke. He had a month's wages coming, and anything Jeanne wanted would be hers. Then, after the movie, it would be straight to Frenchman's Meadows to pick up where they'd left off on their last date. After a few drinks he would once again remind her that he would be going away to college in another month, and that time was running out. They had been going steady for four years, so of course he would respect her afterward; and naturally they *were* going to be married.

His methodical approach to the evening ahead sounded more like tactics than a night out, and that made him feel slightly guilty. But he was up against the Catholic Church, so it was probably guilt by association. Anyway, the guilt was short-lived, drowned in a torrent of testosterone. Tonight he was going to outflank his Eminence. Tonight the Vatican would crumble.

So, the night was set but not certain and it was the uncertainty of it all that was the most compelling. The warm summer winds blew. Three eighteen-year-old boys fueled for a Saturday night, balancing at the edge of manhood and the exciting unknown of the near future. Augmenting their anxiety was the arrival of what had always been, until now, the distant future. For the first time in their lives, each of them had plans that didn't include the other two.

Henry was heading for Alaska. Had his ticket and a job all lined up. He was a quick study, cocksure and ready. He was going to "blow this pop-stand town. Gonna make a little money fer a change."

Jud was off to U.C. Berkeley on a scholarship exchange program with the University of Montana. He was petrified.

Donny was content to "hang out right here in Travers." He stated plainly, "Don't see anything so invitin' about city life. Gonna help my old man on the ranch. Do a little fishin'. And maybe show ol' Dolores the stars."

It was the summer of '64. Travers was home and home was a peaceful setting. There were global problems: a skirmish in some place called Vietnam. Nationally it was racial tensions. But, in rural Montana, things were moving along pretty slow and easy, and the daily news still centered on cattle prices, last night's rain, and what they were biting on. For the most part, at least in Travers Corners, the '60s were just the '50s until '65.

Three young men, straight to the road they had chosen, and no one felt the turning of the wheel. . . .

The Tin Cup was busy. Sarah was behind the grill, her Yankees cap tilted back. She was moving short-order fast. Henry was at his usual stool at the counter having his third cup of coffee, but his first at the cafe. His first one came at four-thirty. His second came after shoeing two horses.

"Morning," Jud said and sat down on a stool, handing the belt sander to Henry.

"Morning," Henry said back and set the sander at his feet.

"All right," Henry said over the brim of his cup, "what did you find last night that is so all-fired important."

Reaching into his shirt pocket, Jud pulled out the photograph and handed it to Henry.

"Well, I'll be dipped!" Henry was pleased, and his usually unreadable and chiseled expression softened into the smile brought on by days gone by.

"This was taken the day that——"

"Excuse me," Henry was interrupted by a man addressing Jud, "but, are you the guy that owns the Boat Works?"

"That's me," Jud answered.

"I hate to bother you, but my brother and I were about to float and fish the river when I found that I had forgotten my oarlocks back in Missoula. Do you have any oarlocks for sale?"

"Sure do."

"Well, I don't want to disturb your breakfast. I . . ."

"Haven't started yet. We can run up the hill and get you a pair. Only take a couple of minutes." Jud stood and took another sip of his coffee. "Henry, order me a couple of eggs, will ya? I'll be right back."

As Jud went out the door with the fisherman, Henry was lost in the old black-and-white, tumbling back to a day long ago and never forgotten, but holding it now in a photograph—the three of them in Old Man Walker's field. His old '51 Ford convertible in the background. That wasn't just any summer's day. . . .

The rush of convertible wind and the roar of glasspacks and the late-afternoon disc jockey on KRNR was in the middle of five in a row from the Beatles: It was summer and the haying was done.

"Hey, stop at McCracken's, will ya? I want to get some coke," Jud said, half-yelling over the pipes and John Lennon.

The Ford rolled to a stop in front of the general store. Henry gave his customary sharp tap to the accelerator, resulting in the desired resonance from his pipes and followed by the precise turning of the key just as the engine was an R.P.M. or two above idle. It was sort of his signature arrival.

Jud and Donny walked past Junior McCracken on the way into the store. He was sitting on the steps eating an ice cream. Junior admired Henry mainly because of his car, without question the coolest car in Travers Corners. Henry took some pleasure watching Junior as he eyeballed the lines of his Ford.

"Hey, Henry."

"Hey, Junior."

"You done hayin' yet?"

"Just now finished," Henry answered as he took a rag from beneath the seat and wiped the dust from the dashboard. He didn't notice Dolores and her cousin, who were following at a distance, coming across Main Street until they had passed the center line.

"Hey, Henry," Dolores said.

Henry liked to have a little time to prepare before dealing with Dolores. It was the time he felt he needed to have his opening line well-rehearsed, to have chosen which wall he would be leaning against when he said it; and then there were all the different ways to hold his face. With no time to summon his cool, Henry was caught short and stammered his reply, "Uh, uh, hey, Dolores."

But, even if Henry had had all the time in the world to prepare his opener, he would have stammered his way through it, for Dolores had all the stops pulled. She had her long brown hair in a ponytail that curled over her shoulders and down the front of her white blouse, open to the last two buttons. Beneath it she had on an overly filled bathing suit top and she was wearing her very short cutoffs, the same pair of cutoffs that had been the subject of much conversation in the hayfields these last three weeks. Her bathing suit, pink, and still wet from her swim, soaked and darkened her blouse, making it cling. Jud bounded down the steps just as a trace of pure hormone was forming on Henry's upper lip.

"Hey, Dolores," Jud greeted.

"Hey, J." Dolores always called Jud "J." She liked the cute way the "hey" and "J." went together. "Where's Donny?"

"He's in buying some stuff," Henry answered, glad for his absence since Dolores always tended to become even dippier than normal when Donny was around. Donny was through the door of McCracken's, a coke and a candy bar in his hands.

"Hey, Donny." Dolores had a way of saying Donny's name that made him sound like he was something good to eat. This drove Henry crazy. He desperately wanted to be in love with Dolores. Dolores desperately wanted to be in love with Donny.

He was six foot four, handsome, with blond hair and blue eyes. He had a certain way about him, a style developed at an early age; in a room full of men his presence would be felt. He was too heavily muscled to be thought of as lanky, but his easy manner and slow gait made him appear so.

Donny could charm any girl in the valley. He could have had Dolores in a heartbeat. However, Donny, like his two friends, remained a virgin for the same reason—different church—that Jeanne did.

Jonathan Boyer, Donny's father, was First Deacon of the First Baptist Church, and imagined himself as the patriarch of the First Family of Travers Corners. The citizen's citizen. Jonathan put the fear of God into his family daily; Sundays it was worse. Damnation and hellfire tripped easily off his tongue, and his political views were quite well known: American flags flew at every corner of the Boyer Ranch, a place where Barry Goldwater was viewed as one from the radical left.

Jud loved Donny as a brother. Henry idolized him. He was the favorite son around Travers Corners; everyone liked him. And according to Lee Wright, regarded as the best fly fisherman in the Elkheart, "He's better than I am, and he's not anywhere as good as he's gonna be. That kid can do things with a fly rod I never seen done."

The girl following Dolores caught up. "Hey, you guys, this is my cousin, Ali. She lives in San Francisco. Remember she came up to visit about eight years ago? Remember I went to see her two years ago?"

Ali looked up at Jud through hair still wet from the swim; it was long and dark and it hung in a drape, hiding half of her face. She had a small freckled nose and big green eyes, like Dolores. But, that's where any resemblances between the cousins ended. Then, there was no resemblance between Ali and anyone who had ever been to, or even passed through, Travers Corners. In spite of the heat, she wore a black turtleneck. She had on strange earrings and weird shoes. She wasn't wearing a bra—a fact that was not lost on any of the boys.

"Hi," Jud said in a slightly sheepish manner. She was like nothing he had ever seen before. She was mysterious, that's what she was; he'd known girls so far to be cute, pretty, perky, down-home, and even sexy, but he'd never met a girl who was mysterious.

She brushed her hair aside and Jud saw the other half of her face. She was only beautiful. He saw her lips part, but her words were drowned out by Henry's turning up the radio.

"She says she loves you and you know you should be glad. Ooooo."

Henry always turned the volume up when the Beatles went "Ooooo." He shook his head, Ringo style, jostling his straw hat until it sat crooked on his head. He did it because it always made Dolores laugh.

Dolores giggled, then pretended to faint by draping herself over the still-open door of the Ford. Henry really didn't care for the Beatles much. He was more of a Ferlin Husky fan.

"Do you like the Beatles?" Jud asked Ali, not knowing what to ask this girl, but feeling the urge to say something.

Distracted, Ali heard the question, but chose to wait a while in her answering. She was looking at the streets of Travers, the front of McCracken's, Henry's Ford, and Junior on the steps, with ice cream down to his wrists. She viewed it all as if it were an exhibit at the Smithsonian. Then slowly she turned to Jud and with an affectation he couldn't place, she answered, "They're okay. I saw them in concert two weeks ago. We had second-row seats."

"WHAT?" Dolores shouted. She couldn't believe that anyone she knew personally, let alone a blood relative, had been second row to Ringo. What she found even harder to believe was that she had been here nearly two days and hadn't told her; finding it out at the same time as everybody else was an act of betrayal from where Dolores stood.

"Father attended a medical conference in London and he took me along. I saw them at the Palladium. But we couldn't hear them for all the young girls screaming. It was like so loud, man," Ali explained in a voice belabored by boredom.

Jud caught himself gawking. He'd never met anyone who had actually seen the Beatles, but, then, he didn't know anyone who'd been to England, either.

Taking an instant dislike to Ali, Henry was angry. How could anyone have seen the Beatles and act as if it had been just another trip to the store? He didn't hold much space for rich people, and it didn't help that she was from California. He believed her about seeing the Beatles, but he wasn't just going to give it to her. "Oh, yeah, sure, and me an' Donny just split a six-pack with Elvis."

Donny and Jud laughed and so did Dolores. Jud just stood there looking at her. No makeup and beautiful.

Shooting a look at Henry, a well-practiced, sophisticated-beyond-her-years look, a look with ice on it, Ali turned to Dolores and with continued blasé said, "While hanging out on the streets of Mayberry with Wally and the Beav promises to be a stone groove, I mean, who knows, in the next hour maybe *another* car might come into town. I'm going back to your crib and listen to some sides. Later." She then turned and started in the direction of Dolores's house.

"Oh, yeah?" Henry was now visibly heated up and sprang to Travers' defense. "Well, who would wanna live in Frisco? What ain't smog is concrete. People crawlin' all over each other. When's the last time you went swimmin' in a river? Hell, you probably didn't even go in—just splashed some water on yer hair."

"Oh, she went swimmin' alright," Dolores said excitedly.

"Then where's yer suit?" Donny asked.

"Didn't wear one," Ali answered, then turned once more, walked past Jud, and, looking up through her hair, smiled the most seductive smile he'd ever seen.

"I'll be along in a minute," Dolores said after her.

The smile sent something within him into motion. He'd never felt anything like it before. It started in his throat and ended in his Levi's, and it twisted everything in its path. She was exotic, and exotic was something he had only seen in magazines. He was so used to Jeanne, who always looked like a Prell commercial; the cheerleader; the virgin homecoming queen, which in fact she was, but it wasn't because he wasn't trying.

But Ali looked like she was fresh from a foreign film. He guessed she had to be a beatnik, but the closest thing he'd ever seen to someone from the beat generation was Maynard G. Krebs, so he didn't have much to go on. He'd read articles on beatniks in *Life* magazine. He'd seen Dave Garroway interview some beatnik poets from San Francisco. Berkeley and San Francisco were practically the same thing. What if most of the people at school are like this? He was going to be a real rube in that world. He could feel his fear of leaving for college rise in his throat. Then he thought of Ali's green eyes, and her breasts, still apparently cool from her swim and outlined in great detail by her turtleneck. He felt another rise, this time against his pocketknife.

As soon as Ali had walked a safe distance, Dolores started wringing her hands and shouting at a whisper, "Oh, you guys, she is soooo strange! I mean I always knew she was a few links short of havin' the full chain, but now . . ." and Dolores rolled her eyes.

"Night before last, after we got back from the airport, me and her are sittin' in my room and she starts telling me how she is sort of livin' with a thirty-year-old writer on a houseboat. She is *only* four months older than me. She has smoked marijuana. She writes poetry, or something that's supposed to be poetry. She read me some; none of it rhymes. And she uses the 'F-word' as freely as a logger. My aunt is really worried about her."

Rattling on as fast as she could, Dolores continued after catching her breath. She was bubbling with embarrassment and at the same time delight, for up to Ali's arrival, it had been summer as usual around Travers Corners. "This mornin' she sat in my room listenin' to her Bob Dylan records and tellin' me over and over to listen to the words. That hillbilly can't sing a lick.

"After lunch, my aunt nearly had to kick her butt before she would go outside and go swimmin'. We git to the crick and she proceeds to git buck-nekid; jumps in; then stretches out on the sand, still not wearin' a stitch, and sunbathes. Old Man Sweeney comes up the river fishin' and just about steps on her. He just about shits his pants and she just lays there like nothin's wrong. She dresses in black all the time. She never laughs. She's always been a spoiled brat."

The thought of Old Man Sweeney stumbling over a naked young woman on the banks of the river had all three of them laughing.

"I gotta go. My mom's jaws are all tight with Ali here. She thinks the devil has a hold on her. My aunt showed her a poem Ali wrote all about her own death, and she is thinkin' that Ali is on the verge of committin' sideways. They don't want me to let her out of my sight. You guys gonna be around tonight?"

"You bet," Henry answered eagerly.

"How about you, Donny?"

"Yeah, me and Henry will be down at Miller's Bridge fishing this evening. We're gonna barbecue some steaks and sample a bit of the Crogans."

"You out with Jeanne tonight, J.?" she asked coyly.

"That's me," Jud answered, but after Ali's smile, he wished he wasn't.

Looking at the clock on McCracken's wall, Jud realized he needed to get back home. He had his mother's car to wash plus some other chores. "Here, you guys, here's my share of the Crogans," he said and fumbled through his pockets for the paper and coin necessary to come in a third on a jar of the moonshine. "I'll meet you down at the river at eight-thirty." Then he grabbed his water jug and shirt from the backseat of the convertible. "Hey Henry. You play your cards right, you might just get to show Ali the stars."

Henry turned the key and flipped Jud the bird; and Donny's laughter could be heard within the rumble of straight pipes and KRNR as the Ford rumbled back out of town.

"Love, love me do. You know I love you. I'll always be true. So please love me do."

As eight o'clock neared, the lights of the Roxy Theater switched on for Saturday night. Jud looked down from his bedroom window to see the splashes of neon from the marquee travel across his mother's Pontiac, still wet from the wash and parked in the driveway. He paced between the window and his mirror, stopping at the mirror with each pass to check out his new shirt and new Levi's. From his window he could read the marquee. In broken, black, red, and missing letters, it read:

HUd
STArRinG
PAul NewbURg anD PAtriCia Neeley
9 o'clOK ONly

Normally, Jud handled putting up the letters on the marquee, but during haying season Mr. Parrish did it himself; and now his knowledge of the current cinema played for all to see.

Jud imagined his mother already at the candy counter, popping up the evening's popcorn. Soon she would be opening the doors, selling the tickets, helping at the candy counter. Later she would do the book work. She'd been working at the Roxy for Mr. Parrish for nine years, working weekends and summers, her second job behind teaching fourth grade. The two jobs were necessary, because college, even now with a scholarship, was going to be a stretch. A lump formed in his throat, the fear of college and the city, the fear of failure. But he took one more look in the mirror and replaced the fear by once again going over tonight's itinerary: movie; ice cream; Frenchman's Meadows; coke, ice, Crogans. He'd be leaving for college in just a month, he'd love her afterward even more, et cetera.

He went down the steps, twirling the keys to the Pontiac on his finger. He could feel the night's excitement traveling as something electric down the length of his skin. This was the night. He looked across the street to the Roxy. Tonight there would be some necking in the balcony, but very little. It made Jud uncomfortable to make out at the movies with his mother just downstairs. But, the necking in Frenchman's Meadows was going to be serious. He thought of Jeanne, but he couldn't get Ali's turtleneck out of his mind.

It was eight thirty-one as Jud motored toward Brown's Bridge. The disc jockey had just given him the exact time and now he was giving him the new one from the Beatles—"She was just seventeen, do ya know what I mean? And the way she looked was way beyond compare."

It was eight thirty-one and Henry was flying down the old highway. He'd picked up the Crogans and had sampled it straight from the jar. He was driving fast and imagining breasts. Dolores's breasts. Maybe tonight would be his night. Maybe tonight Dolores will let him show her the stars. Maybe: All his hopes balanced on the word. But, if ever there was a night where a maybe could happen, it was this night. He could taste it, and the savory sweetness of his daydreams went well with the moonshine.

"Well, my heart went boom when I crossed that room and I held her hand in mine. Oooooo."

It was eight thirty-one and Donny was already at the bridge. He was knee-deep in the Elkheart and had been taking trout with alarming regularity since he'd arrived an hour before; and the hatch was just beginning. He'd spent the evening before tying flies, and his flies were a perfect match. The big fish were up. There was something in the air tonight; he could feel it. He'd seen evenings like this on the river before, but rarely.

"Well, I'll never dance with another, o-o-o-o, since I saw her standing there."

It was eight thirty-one when Henry, followed by Jud, drove across Brown's Bridge. The bridge was posted: ONE-VEHICLE LIMIT, but Henry and Jud always tried to cross it together; it was just another one of their ways to defy gravity, but they also enjoyed defying signs of any kind. The heavy timbers twisted and rumbled beneath their tires, reducing the music, though at full volume in both Pontiac and Ford, to a joyful background rhythm. The river danced and the trout were rising. Donny knew this was going to be such a night of fishing. His spirits were soaring. He made another cast.

It was eight thirty-one and the evening—though calm and cooling after the day's heat, serene from all that is fly fishing, and tranquil with the old bridge and its setting—still managed to have an edge on it. The river's gentle murmur was lost under all the rock and roll. To what heights the night would take them there was no way of knowing, but something was up and they were being told by the collective crawling of their skins.

It was eight thirty-one. There was still an hour of daylight left, but according to the metaphysical timepiece, whose mainspring had just been wound by a celestial hurricane, it was nighttime. It was Saturday nighttime. And the boys, though they could sense it, had no way of knowing that tonight all the comets were flying in formation, and that many of the riddles were soon to be not only answered but rhymed.

Click. It was eight thirty-two. . . .

"Hey, that's what I call timing," Jud said, sitting back down at the counter as Sarah brought his breakfast order out from the grill. Jud's return gave Henry a start, and for a moment he appeared a little disoriented. Jud was simply returning to the Tin Cup from a trip up the hill. Henry was returning to the cafe from thirty years ago.

"You gotta remember the day that was taken?"

"I can barely remember last week, but I can remember that night like this was the followin' mornin'. You know who's gotta see this?"

"Dolores?"

"Yep."

"I'm going to stop by the beauty parlor and show it to her on the way home."

Henry looked at the clock on the wall. "Hey, I gotta git," he said, standing. "Lots to do today. I want a copy of that picture. Did you notice my old Ford back by the corral?"

"Yeah."

"See ya."

"See ya, Henry," and Jud returned to his breakfast.

Sarah came out from behind the grill, sat down next to Jud, and picked up the photograph. "Well, would you look at you two," she laughed.

"Who's the boy in the middle?"

"That's Donny. You've heard Henry and me talk about Donny before?"

"Oh sure, he was the boy who was . . ."

"Excuse me, I am sorry to bother you again." It was the lawyer from before. "But it seems, upon closer inspection, in addition to the oarlocks, we seem to have forgotten the oars as well. We'll need to buy a pair. But please enjoy your breakfast. We'll just wait for you up at the Boat Works."

Caught with a mouthful of hash browns, Jud just nodded his answer and the fisherman left. "A couple of fishermen from Helena," Jud explained to Sarah. "In a couple of minutes they'll probably be back in to tell me they have also forgotten their boat. Lawyers. They're slick, clever, and shrewd, but take them out of the courtroom and they're useless."

Sarah laughed, then returned to the grill. Jud left the money on the counter for his meal and headed not for the Boat Works, but to Dolores' as planned. The door to the beauty parlor was open and inside, pinned on the wall, was a note that read: "Back In Five Minutes." Normally, he would have waited the five minutes; but this was Dolores, and with Dolores five minutes could be an hour. He took down the note and wrote below it: "This was taken the afternoon of that night at Brown's Bridge." He then pinned the photograph and note back on the wall.

He walked back to the Boat Works at a leisurely pace; there was something about making a pair of lawyers wait that pleased him.

When she returned, the photograph was the first thing Dolores saw. She pulled it from the wall and read Jud's note. She sat down slowly, looking at the three boys, and easily envisioned that night down by the river. . . .

Holding the jar of Crogans above his head, Henry was dancing in his seat as he parked the Ford just as Donny missed the trout he had been trying for. So naturally, Henry was the first to initiate the insults and yelled,

"Hey, you can't catch fish. You're way too ugly." Henry then became aware of the numbers of fish coming up to the mayflies on the water. He was instantly out of the Ford and grabbed his fly rod and irrigation boots. He paused only to watch Donny take another nice rainbow; then, once again, there was thunder on the bridge.

Henry looked up to see Dolores and Ali, in Dolores' father's pickup. Dolores jumped out of the truck and shouted down, "Did you yahoos manage to scare up some of the Crogans?"

Henry hollered back, "We got a jarful." He was slipping on hip-boots and looking up at Dolores, who was leaning over the bridge and wearing a low-cut red blouse; and even though he was fifteen feet below, her cleavage wasn't lost on him: a plunging neckline—and he was a boy who was up to taking the plunge.

The sun was setting, now about half-hidden behind the mountains. Dolores was half out of her top, Henry's shirt was half-soaked in testosterone, Ali was out of the car and halfway down the bridge, Jud was halfway down the path under the bridge, and Donny was working his way upstream. He was about half the distance he needed to be to make a cast for a very, very large trout. Half would be the last fraction for the night.

Ali, still dressed in North Beach black, barefoot, and disinterested to the point of disdain in anything happening downstream, leaned over the opposite railing just as Jud walked around a bend in the willowed path. Her sudden shadow crossed his way and startled him and he jerked back as if to dodge a falling object. He looked up at the soft long hair, those big green eyes, and the same black turtleneck from that afternoon. "Uh, hi there, Ali. You kinda gave me a start there."

"The river, flowing goddess,/ we worship you all too seldom./ Your quiet undulations breathe/ reason within my soul," Ali replied.

It wasn't your "Hi, how-ya-doing?" kind of hello. He'd never heard a girl say "undulations" before, and it unnerved him. "Oh, you can just call me Jud, if you like," he said, then nervously laughed at his own joke.

Ali almost laughed herself, but she caught herself and maneuvered her smile back into a pouty sneer. She returned to her role of off-beat and distant. She was still wavering under the strains of her newfound womanhood, and she'd chosen, at least for now, the Joan Baez approach. Laughing was for everybody else, such a bourgeois reaction. But her smile had betrayed her. She tried to cover the girl within her behind an emotionless face; delight was definitely against the code of the truly hip. "I think people should meet each other with poetry." She was stretching, even for her, but this hayseed had just made her smile, and being as weird as you can get didn't include anything like happiness.

"I liked your poem," Jud said, working his smile. "I write a little poetry myself." The admission surprised him. Writing poetry was something he had kept hidden from Henry and Donny for obvious reasons, but he hadn't even told Jeanne. Now five seconds into their second meeting he had shared one of his secrets, and at eighteen he didn't have many, with this mysterious girl with the green eyes and the turtleneck.

"I write poetry every day. I . . ."

Ali was interrupted by Donny, who was yelling like a rodeo cowboy, and it echoed down the river and amplified beneath the bridge.

"Yaaaaaa-hooooo!"

Immersed in Dolores' hooters, Henry, busy pulling his right hip boot on to his left foot, had missed the first jump, but he turned in time to see the second. The rainbow was instantly realized as the trout of a lifetime. He mimicked Donny's yell: "Yaaaaa-hooooo!"

Dolores let out a shriek. She didn't know much about fishing. But she knew she had just seen a really big fish. She began yelling and running along the bridge. Yelling the way she did for Donny in football. She wanted Donny to win. She wanted Donny.

The commotion sent Jud running down the path. He couldn't see through the willows what was causing all the excitement, but he knew there was a large fish on. Donny always gave his rodeo yell when he hooked into a big one. But a fish that would cause Henry to holler as well, and to make Dolores scream?

Moving fast through the willows and over an uneven trail, Jud didn't consider the extra length in his new dress boots and misjudged an exposed root just as the path began to run downhill.

After tumbling to a stop, Jud found himself up to his hip pockets in a small, marshy backwater. It had been the complete fall: pants ripped, shirt torn, his boots filled with swamp water. He then realized he had cut his hand as well. It didn't hurt too much but the blood mixed with water made it look life-threatening.

"Yeeee-haaaaaa!" The yell brought him back to his feet and he broke out of the willows on a dead run, water and mud squirting from his boots.

In the middle of the river he could see Donny, hands high, his rod bent double and scrambling from the deeper water to the shore, loping through the current, water spraying in all directions. The fish was on a long and powerful run. Donny finally made it to shore just as his line was winding down to the final wraps. He chased after his fish. The rainbow would have easily distanced an older angler, but at eighteen, Donny made it a contest.

Henry was now running alongside him, his right boot on his left foot, the other foot bare, and shouting, "Don't let 'er git into them snags!"

Ali joined Dolores on the downstream side of the bridge. Dolores was bouncing up and down, screaming, "It's a really big one! It's a really, really big one!" Ali, oncc she realized that all the hoopla was about a fish, went about trying to spot Jud—the reason for crossing the bridge in the first place. But, all she could see was the top of his head through all the underbrush, and she wasn't sure, but it looked like there were leaves stuck in his hair.

The fish was in the air again. A great silvered leap, twisting and shimmering in the last light of the day. This time everyone saw it. Jud took off running and soon was alongside the other two. Henry looked over, half running and half hobbling. "What happened to you?"

"I had a wreck in the willows. Did you see the size of that fish?!!"

"Yeah, bigger than anything I ever saw before!"

The fish stopped just short of going under the bridge, resting in the deep pool just below. It was a pool filled with old snags, and pilings from an even older bridge. "Keep 'er away from the snags!" Henry shouted his instructions once more, this time more for Dolores' benefit. He was insuring, in the event that Donny somehow landed the fish, that he would be remembered as his angling advisor.

Donny knew he was going to lose the fish. It was just too much trout.

From the bridge the two girls could see the trout clearly as it struggled near the surface. "It's as big as the fish on the wall at McCracken's!" Dolores shouted.

It was easily one of the most beautiful creatures Ali had ever seen as it moved near the surface not ten feet below her. Suddenly, the rainbow, perhaps startled by Dolores' movements, circled downward to be lost in the depths. Donny played her gently, as gently as he could, but if she wanted to head into the willows, there would be nothing he could do to stop her. He applied a little pressure, trying to turn her head, when she erupted from the river once more, throwing water like welder's work. She made a sharp run back into the current, making another leap, which looked more like an unintentional departure from the river than a jump, brought about by sheer speed. She then turned and headed straight back for the submerged deadfall.

The trout was lost in the riverglare, but Donny could feel that she had wrapped the line. He would lose her to a snag. "She's dallied herself!"

"Dallied herself" meant nothing to Ali. She shot a look at Dolores looking for a translation. "What's going to happen to the fish?"

Dolores was quick to respond. She'd been waiting for her chance to know something this beatnik didn't know ever since she arrived. "The fish has wrapped itself around a branch or somethin'," she explained. Then, sensing that Ali's concern was for the fish, and not the fisherman, she added, "When that happens they almost always die." Dolores, of course, didn't know what she was talking about, for all a fish this size need do to break off would be to simply nod its head.

From the bridge Ali could trace Donny's line to the root of the problem, a cottonwood root to be more precise. The line was caught on the snag just below the surface, and it was held in the current like a bowstring. She couldn't see the trout.

Positive now that he wouldn't be landing the fish, Donny was glad to have had some eyewitnesses, and what better bystanders could there have been than his two best friends and fishing partners. They wouldn't have believed him if they hadn't seen it. Nobody would. Donny's mind was racing for a solution. He gave subtle twitches to the line in the hopes the fish might get aggravated and accidentally free itself.

It was obvious at once, to both Henry and Jud, what had to be done. One of them was going to have to go for a swim, to follow Donny's line and free it from its tangle. Jud, the stronger swimmer of the two, ran upstream to get a better angle on the snag. But before he could slip out of his second boot, the splash of Ali's dive into the river was heard, and all that could be seen were the waves of her entry. Dolores looked on the bridge behind her at a pile of rumpled black clothes.

Swimming confidently underwater, Ali's pale figure came to Jud through the fractured sunlight on the surface, and it reflected off her white skin like a moving mosaic, like an alabaster dancer by Picasso done in liquid light. Her long hair pulsed in the currents. She turned on her side as she plucked the line free of the root, then she burst to the surface for air and floated with the current into the shadows where her limbs appeared as creamy, willowy distortions. Jud was hypnotized.

"Yeeeeee-haaaaaaa."

Donny first felt slack in his line, and his heart sank, but stripping it in, he found himself taut to the rainbow once more. The trout took off on another blistering run; this time downstream. Donny surged from the river and the chase continued, Henry right at his side, shouting "Keep her nose up."

Ali was treading water, heading for the shallows. She was looking at Jud and from her look, almost a dare, it was apparent there would be no hesitation—due to a mere lack of clothing—to her getting out. The prospective nudity made him both embarrassed and excited, but embarrassment prevailed and he turned and ran, following the fight. He ran looking over his shoulder, hoping that he might see something. But just as Ali was starting her climb to the shore, Dolores, down from the bridge, jumped in front of her, shoving Ali's clothing into her arms.

There was no way in the world Dolores would have taken her clothes off in front of all those boys and she nearly contorted at the very thought of it. "You can't do that kind of shit, girl. Goin' skinny dippin' with the girls is one thing, but gettin' buck nekid in front of those three yahoos—well, you are just askin' for it."

(*Author's note:* Most of you will remember the *it* to which Dolores was referring. *It* served as the teenage euphemism for the sexual act in the early '60s. *It*, promiscuity's very own pronoun; *it*, the subject of eighty percent of all adolescent conversation—"I think they are doing *it*, I hear she does *it*, have you done *it*?" *It* was the mystery that made your mouth water. *It* separated the men from the boys. Of course, by the late '60s, *it* was the subject of revolution.)

It was something Ali had tried and liked, whereas *it* remained something that Dolores would like to try.

Slipping on her turtleneck and pants, Ali grabbed Dolores by the hand. "Come on. We have to stop them from killing that fish."

The trout had moved into a long stretch of deep water around the bend. Donny had chased the fish a hundred yards, but the rainbow was beginning to tire; her age and weight were working against her. Donny played the fish beautifully, with the finesse and patience usually found in an older angler. Slowly, thoughtfully, certainly reverently, Donny eased the fish into the shallows. This was the fish of a lifetime. There could be no mistakes.

Henry was working his way in behind the great trout; netless, he was hoping to tail the fish. Jud, behind him, looked on. With their backs upstream, lost in the final moments of the fight, the fish beginning to list on her side in submission, the three were unaware of the sudden appearance of Ali with Dolores in her bright red blouse. The colorful arrival might have been lost on the boys, but the blouse was not lost on the rainbow. This sudden surge of color stirred something within the trout, something within the primal dictates of survival, summoning the fight she still had in her and some she didn't. She suddenly began to thrash and roll, then hurled herself lengthwise above the Elkheart; a second wind blew from deep within. One last short, desperate run, and she was lost.

Henry made a dive for her but missed as her brilliant silver-and-crimson flanks ghosted slowly into deep water; one last pearly twist of light, a glint, and she was gone.

For a moment there was silence as a pall of disbelief set in, broken finally by Henry. "We came so close." Henry was now looking at the trout, and the fight to land her, as if they belonged to him, and Jud as well; after all, they were right there with him every inch of the way—just as always.

They didn't fix the blame on Dolores; none of them realized the correlation of the red blouse and losing the rainbow. It was viewed simply as a wily old trout's last-ditch effort, which worked. Donny let out a deep sigh. He felt a tightness in his throat and sick to his stomach, but he fought it by suggesting, "I think I could use a shot of the Crogans."

Then everyone began talking and shouting at once as they walked backed to the cars. "Well, you almost had her, Donny . . . Yeah, you played 'er well, couldn't of played 'er any better myself. How big was it? Ten pounds . . . twelve pounds . . . fifteen pounds, easy. . . . She was so big . . . a monster. Maybe twenty-eight inches long . . . Twenty-nine or thirty, no problem. Over thirty inches for sure . . . I should have played her longer. . . . If Ali hadn't of freed the line, Donny would've lost her back at the bridge. . . . I wasn't trying to free the line, I was trying to free the fish."

"YOU WERE WHAT?!" Henry yelled, nearly screaming.

"I was trying to free the fish. It was much too beautiful to kill," Ali explained slowly and with a puzzled look, wondering how Henry could have questioned the obvious.

"That there was a trophy. We'll fish the rest of our lives and none of us will ever see a fish like that again," Henry said scratching his head, then looked over to Jud. "City chicks."

But, Henry's comment went unnoticed by Ali, as she had just caught sight of the blood on Jud's shirt sleeve, and the wound. "Jud," she said, reaching for his hand, "that's a bad cut. I think you should have stitches."

"Hell, ain't no more than a scratch," Henry disagreed.

"This is a deep cut," Ali explained, still holding Jud's hand, "and I am sure it could use two or three stitches."

"How do you know?" Henry challenged.

"My father is a doctor."

"That don't make you a doctor."

Stepping in for a closer look, Donny, in his slow and deliberate manner, judged, "Well, it looks kinda like one of those cuts that better be stitched or just bandaged real well. I got a first-aid kit in the truck. We can disinfect it with a little Crogans."

"You ain't gonna waste perfectly good Crogans on a little scratch?" Henry protested.

So, while Henry and Donny built a fire, talking constantly about the trout, reliving the fight over and over again, Dolores organized the paper plates, the beans, and the steaks, and Ali tended to Jud's hand. As she bandaged, Ali was doing her best to impress him with her newly formed and radical politics, and her constantly evolving philosophies. Jud was infatuated; she sounded so smart, and so she should have. She was quoting Kerouac verbatim.

The first ration of Crogans was used sparingly and medicinally. The next measures of the moonshine flowed freely and in less than an hour a weekend's worth of Crogans was nearly gone, when once again there was thunder on the bridge. Saturday night was coming up to speed.

It was Jeanne in her mother's new Cadillac stopping just behind Dolores's truck, still on the bridge. So much had happened in the last hour; it was only then Jud realized just how late he was for his date. He would have some serious explaining to do. But the scene from the bridge, lit by bonfire, told Jeanne everything she needed to know: Henry, weaving his way around the camp; Donny smiling his silly drunken smile, sitting at the edge of the river; Dolores sitting at the edge of Donny; rock and roll on the radios; and Jud, her four-year steady, the man envisioned in her dowries and dreams, sitting on a log holding hands with Dolores' creepy cousin. His hand hadn't left hers since the bandaging.

Jeanne went into a rage. She slammed the Caddy into reverse, she stomped on the accelerator. Unfortunately, the reverse in the new car was where low had been in the old one. The clashing of metal and the tinkling of glass echoed off the bridge and down the river. Dolores' old pickup, hardly dented from the impact, lunged forward; but the Caddy had been hurt.

Too furious to be daunted, Jeanne found reverse and flew backward. Steam spewed from the Caddy's radiator, and part of the grill dragged in the dirt. It took three tries to turn the long de Ville around on the narrow county road; but once around, she was away in a fishtail. Her dust drifted through the willows. The roar of the engine was soon only a distant hum.

To Henry the whole show was better than television: Jeanne's trashing her old lady's new Cadillac. Henry didn't really like Jeanne. He thought she was a snob, called her Queenie Jeannie when Jud wasn't around, and didn't care for her father, the banker, either. He was laughing so hard he could no longer stand and fell over backward into the sand. This set Donny to laughing, and when Donny laughed, the rest couldn't help joining in, including Ali, who laughed louder than anyone.

Jud felt torn. Should he chase after Jeanne, the girl he'd gone with forever; the girl who, after hundreds of hours of necking, would only let him under one side of her bra; the girl who couldn't take any more than two sips of the Crogans without faking an upchuck; the girl who always drug the Vatican along when he wanted to show her the stars?

Or, should he stay with Ali, the girl with the big green eyes, who was drinking freely, open to nudity, and an admitted atheist? No contest.

The winds of chance were spiraling. Fate would soon be a funnel cloud; touchdown—Travers Corners. . . .

After Jud had dealt with the lawyers, selling them the oars they needed, he walked back into town for the mail. He stopped by the beauty parlor to pick up the photograph. There sat Dolores in her operator's chair, the old photograph still in her hand, her hand on her lap, and sound asleep.

As he knocked on the screen door and opened it, Dolores was slow to wake. "Oh, geez, Jud. I must'a drifted off. Margie Morris was supposed to be my nine-o'clock but she's come down with some kind of a bug and had to cancel." She looked at her watch. "I must'a been out a good half hour." Then she held up the photo. "Where did ya ever find this?"

"Fell out of a book last night."

"Has Henry seen it?"

"Show'd it to him this morning over coffee."

Handing him the photograph, Dolores said, "Thanks for bringing it by. Sure brought back a lot of memories. Nineteen sixty-four seems like a long time ago, but just now it seems like yesterday. God, were we ever that young?"

"I barely remember it myself sometimes, but here's proof," Jud said, holding up the old photograph. "And Dolores, you're just as pretty now, prettier even, than in 1964." Jud winked. "Gotta run." He really didn't have to run, but the smell of the beauty parlor always made him nauseated.

He was heading for McCracken's and the morning mail, but he ducked down Dolores' alley to the path that runs along the river; he wanted to take a look at the Elkheart and see how it was holding up under all this heat and no rain. He leaned over the rail at Town Bridge and stared into the river. His thoughts flowed back easily to that time; it was a time he had thought of often over the years. It was the time no one ever forgets, the first time. . . .

"Hey, we're all out of the Crogans," Henry lamented, "and that ain't no way to be."

So, it was decided: Dolores, Donny, and Henry would go for another jar of the moonshine and then into town for more Coke and some ice. Ali, with Jud, chose to stay behind, and as soon as Henry's Ford rumbled out of earshot, Ali suggested, "Let's go for a swim." Then she leaned in and kissed him. She kissed him once. He'd never been kissed like that before. She pulled at his belt buckle, then backing toward the river, she first took off the turtleneck, and then her pants—with the same moral ease as someone kicking off their shoes. He was out of his clothes just as quickly, his speed brought on by embarrassment as he was pointing out his intentions to join her without the use of his hands. Nothing like this had happened to him before, nothing even close to this. Things like this didn't happen in Travers Corners—not to him, anyway.

"The air is so wonderful. I feel so free tonight," she shouted into the night, then dove into the water, Jud right behind her.

She swam effortlessly around him, teasing him with light touches as she glided past. Swimming unseen beneath the water, she encircled him. He could feel the currents caused by her movements as she came from the depths, sliding her body along his. He looked down to see beads of air stringing from the corners of her mouth. Her limbs wound around his and she kissed him long and hard.

"I'm getting a little cold," she said. "Let's go somewhere and get warm."

"Back by the fire?"

"No, I want to go someplace else."

"But, what about the others, the Crogans and stuff?"

"No, let's get out of here."

With the radio dialed to rock and roll, they drove to Frenchman's

Meadows, and that night, under a moon that was hung for the howling, under the endless summer sky, in the warm July air, on the front seat, in the backseat, on a blanket in the grass, Ali not only showed Jud the stars, she defined them. . . .

A cattle truck rolled onto Town Bridge, shaking Jud free from his first-time memory. He headed for McCracken's and the mail. He walked slowly, smiling the smile of the morning after, even though that Saturday night had been nearly thirty years ago.

Then he was back at the Boat Works where he spent the remainder of the day doing finishing work, sanding mostly, on two boats he needed to have ready by next week. He also ordered more oars and oarlocks in the hopes another pair of lawyers would be coming to town to row the river. All day long he couldn't get that Saturday out of his mind—how the night turned into something so incredible for him, while Donny, Henry, and Dolores were engaged in an evening of a different kind. . . .

The Crogans secured, Henry's Ford was flat out and roaring down the indigo highway. With McCracken's closed, they parked in front of the Tin Cup Bar and Henry alone headed in for the Coke and ice. But when Donny saw Lee Wright's truck out front, he joined him. He was busting to tell someone about the great trout; and Lee, his fly fishing mentor, was the one person he needed to tell. Dolores, then, came along as well, since she was busting to tell anyone and everyone about the great breakup of Jud and Jeanne.

In the Tin Cup sat the usual crowd, but they were favoring the end of the bar by the jukebox. For at the other end sat Mean. He barely looked up as the three came through the swinging doors. George Meaney was his name, but around Travers he was known simply as Mean. He was a loner who came to town only occasionally. He came to get drunk. He came to fight. The regulars knew this, and they gave him plenty of room. For an unintentional look would be all the excuse Mean needed to beat a man senseless.

Stepping up to the rail, midway between the regulars and Mean, Henry placed his order for Coke and ice with Slim, who was tending bar. Henry, full of the Crogans and feeling bulletproof, looked down at Mean to show him that he held little regard for Mean's reputation. He did this mostly to impress Dolores. His bravado was lost on Dolores, however, for she was leaning in with Lee and the regulars as Donny started his tale. But, Henry's defiance didn't go unnoticed by Mean, who slowly returned to staring into his whiskey.

"Did some fishin' tonight, Lee," Donny began, "down at Brown's Bridge." Donny understood the protocol involved in telling a fish story and the sequences all anglers hold in abeyance. First comes the setup: the location and the time. Second, the details: hatches and conditions. Third, the fight: starting with the spotting of the trout, through the ensuing battle, to the net. Finally, you conclude with the particulars: the size and weight of the trout. For most fish, the story is enough. But, when the rainbow is a trophy, you really need to produce the trout for credibility. Fortunately, he had witnesses, one of whom decided to skip ahead to the bottom line.

"Donny caught the biggest fish ever. Bigger than the one on the wall at McCracken's," Dolores blurted out.

"So bring it on in here," Lee said excitedly and the regulars agreed.

"Well, uh, it kinda got away," Donny said sheepishly. The tale is in the telling, but like a joke whose punchline has been spoiled, his story had just been robbed of its art. Backtracking through a fish story taints its credibility, so he called in his second witness. "Tell 'em Henry."

"Bigger than the one on the wall at McCracken's. Bigger by a couple'a inches," Henry verified. He was feeling a rage building inside him. An anger brought on by Dolores' fawning all over Donny. It was jealousy, a jealousy he could do nothing about. Donny was his best friend. He wasn't sure, but he was pretty sure, that he was in love with Dolores.

"Bullshit," Mean hollered from his end of the bar and took a half-turn on his stool. He now sat facing Henry but was looking right through him to Donny.

Mean looked his name. A bull of a man, ill-kept, skin flecked with dirt, and wearing the same flannel shirt and bib overalls he'd been seen in forever. His beard was greasy and stained from spitting tobacco. "You young punks been drinking Crogans shine and ya think you can come in here and bullshit us, 'cause you got nothin' to do 'cept drive around and play with that little slut's titties."

The others at the bar just left it alone. Dolores started to cry. It was the spark Henry needed for ignition. He could barely see Mean through the white light of his own insanity and the haze from the Crogans. He struck like a snake. His fist landed, powered by all the strength he could gather. It was a well-timed, dead-center, full-swing, and surprisingly accurate punch that landed in the middle of Mean's piglike face, and blood instantly flowed from his nose; but that was the blow's only effect. Mean laughed, then came at Henry, grabbing him by the neck and throwing him to the floor. Then he picked up a stool and brought it down on Henry with the force to kill. Henry instinctively raised his arm to block the blow, and above the shouting of the regulars and the twang of the jukebox, came the crack of breaking bones.

"Someone go get Doc Higgins," Slim shouted as he reached for the phone.

Coming through two empty tables charged Donny. Hitting Mean waist-high, driving him through a hat rack, a cart of empty glasses, and into the wall. Mean struck back with two heavy blows to Donny's head, knocking him to one knee. Slim shouted down the phone to the Sheriff's office, "Get a deputy down here!"

Mean tried to kick Donny, but Donny grabbed his leg and drove him through the open door and into the street. Mean was fighting because he enjoyed inflicting pain. Donny was fighting because of what Mean had done to Henry. This wasn't a barnyard scuffle with his best friend—to this moment, the only fighting Donny had ever done—this was a barroom brawl and now a street fight with the most feared man in the valley. Lee Wright and the regulars, with Dolores screaming and crying, followed. Slim stayed with Henry.

The fight continued for what seemed like hours, perhaps because of its repetitiveness: Donny would get knocked down and kicked, but then would somehow manage to get up only to tackle Mean again. Sometimes he rammed Mean with so much power that he would lift him from the ground, driving him into the nearest structure. Mean was bounced off parked cars, walls, a maple tree, and a stop sign.

Donny was losing. He was cut and bleeding. Mean hit him again. Donny charged Mean once more, but this time clothes-lining him, slamming him headlong into the street light on the corner of First and Main. His head struck the hollow metal standard with a sound one could easily liken to the ring of hammer meeting anvil. The clang echoed up and down Main Street, and those who hadn't already been awakened by the fight as it pinballed its way around town were now switching on their lights and coming to their windows.

At first Mean was thought to be dead. He was out cold for nearly an hour, and when he regained consciousness he was cuffed and taken to jail.

Henry was taken away in an ambulance, while Doc Higgins stitched up the cuts on Donny's eyes and Dolores nearly dried up from crying—and, unaware of the mayhem in town, all alone in the woods, Jud and Ali were seeing nothing but stars. . . .

Jud worked late into the evening, his finish work never quite being finished. A summer rain tapped on the tin roof of the workshop. The rain came as a surprise; so locked into his work, he was unaware of the clouds and the wind that brought it. As he put away his tools, the aftermath of that Saturday night played over and over in his mind—how one crazy and reckless evening had changed so many things, and how it all had started with Donny's father.

Jonathan Boyer was ashamed and humiliated by the actions of his boy: fighting in the street, drunk, the whole town watching, the day before the Sabbath. The embarrassment this brought to the family and the church was more than the good Deacon could bear. So, he did what was right for his boy. He made him atone for his sins. He made him fulfill his Christian obligations. He made Donny join the army.

Everyone has an image of Vietnam. It may be a famous photograph, such as the little girl screaming, burned by napalm; or one may envision the Memorial, the long black wall of too many names. For Jud it was the memory of coming home to Travers Corners, almost a year after that Saturday night, standing in the heat at the train station along with everyone else in town, waiting to meet Donny in his coffin.

He wondered, as pieces of that horrible day played before his mind's eye, what would have happened if one little thing had been different on that night: if Henry hadn't punched Mean, if Mean hadn't been in town, if he and Ali would have gone on the Crogans run. If . . .

If, the errant chalk mark; if, the chameleon in the lexicon; if, the wind-blown conditional.

If everything that happens has a purpose, if there is indeed a reason for all things, then that Saturday night, even the fight, senseless as it was, had its resolute moments in destiny: if Mean hadn't shattered Henry's arm, an arm that to this day still won't straighten out all the way, then Henry wouldn't have been classified 4-F; if the bitter truth of Vietnam hadn't been driven home so dramatically by Donny's death, Jud, who was in his third quarter, on probation, and teetering at the edge of flunking out, might not have buckled down—studying to stay in school, studying to stay out of the war.

He thought of the others involved in that Saturday night. Dolores, she's doing fine. She dressed down and grew up a bit after that Saturday night. She married Henry; it didn't work out, but they remain close friends, *very* close friends. Mean disappeared; it's rumored he was murdered. Why couldn't Mean have gone to Vietnam instead of Donny? Mean loved to fight. But he was too old, and anyway, because of his prison record, he just would have been classified as I-V: too violent to go to war.

And Ali, well, Jud never saw her again. Dolores stays in touch. She ended up marrying a wealthy businessman and she's still politically active. Dolores says she has just started a foundation to give the homeless jobs collecting handguns at abortion clinics.

"*If*—the fisherman's conjunction," Jud said aloud and smiled a bit. "The fishing will be good tomorrow, if the wind doesn't blow, if the mayflies come out, if it doesn't rain, if it does rain, if it's not too hot, if it's not too cold, if the creeks don't rise, and if the trout are willing." He turned out the lights and headed for the house. Annie the Wonderlab nuzzled his hand as he walked. Jud bent down and gave her a rub on her ears. "If only Donny had landed that rainbow, Annie, he would be around and fishing with us still."

7

Pastime

LIKE EVERYTHING THAT gains in the aging—whiskey, memories, and women—angling, his angling anyway, had improved over the years. And Jud wasn't thinking about his skills as a fisherman, since he was certain any proficiencies acquired and refined had undergone subtle losses now that he stood on the lee side of fifty.

He was in his apron, up at the Boat Works, hand-working some stubborn cedar in the workshop, and reviewing his life as an angler. . . .

He'd gone through all the stages all young men must. In his teens he knew all a man needed to know about fly fishing. In his twenties he tried to learn all the things he hadn't needed to know, as well as all the things he'd thought he knew only the decade before. He also treated fly fishing as a sport. Fly fishing isn't a sport; basketball is a sport.

In his thirties he went about fine-tuning his love of fishing, collecting the arcane and completing the scientific filigree. This was all fine and well, and enjoyable on a cold January night; tying flies, wrapping rods, and reading Haig Brown. But all these endeavors are only the periphery, simple wintertime diversions, indoor amusements. But fly fishing isn't a parlor game; Monopoly is a parlor game.

And now, thirty-odd years a fly fisherman, he could say that his angling continues to amend. Sure, some of this betterment could be attributed to all those long winter nights of study, as well as to three decades of practiced dedication, but mostly these enhancements could be attributed to the people he had met along the way, specifically those people he had met through guiding. It was from those fishermen, almost always older people, as older folks have a tendency to distill everything down to its essence, that he came to know what fly fishing really is: one of life's most pleasant pastimes and nothing more. Nothing more, because there are few things more fulfilling than a pleasant pastime.

(*Author's note:* Now there will be some readers who disagree, thinking that I have just reduced something regarded by many of you as a passion down to a pastime. Please allow me to defend my reasoning in the following pages. But, dear reader, know that: this is not a yarn; this is not a story; this is not a fable tucked away in the long list of allegories that is the fiction of Travers Corners. This is a simple and true tale; and as with most tales that are more than twice-told, it holds a lesson.)

His chisel had grown dull and Jud walked over to the stone on the workbench. He then grabbed two other chisels, as an afterthought, thinking that if he was going to sharpen the one, he might as well do them all. It was a cold spring afternoon, a good day for mindless work and reminiscing. It was fifteen years ago, fifteen years this coming summer. . . .

Jud had just stepped outside the Boat Works for some fresh air. It was hot and strangely humid, strange since humidity was rare in the Elkheart. A dog day, which really isn't bad duty if you've ever watched a dog on a hot day. Annie the Wonderlab knew a dog day when she saw it and was stretched out in the shadiest part of the yard. The leaves on his apple tree flickered as the stirrings of a welcome breeze kicked up a little dust on the drive.

From the Boat Works he could see the kids running around down on Main Street, armed with squirt guns and water balloons. Some of the locals were pulling into the Tin Cup, and happy hour would be starting a little earlier than normal—the heat and all. Clouds began to form around the summit of Mt. D. Downey.

The Elkheart hadn't been fishing well for a week; five straight days in the nineties, but if cloud cover came in this afternoon, the fishing this evening could be quite good.

Hearing the sound of a car, he turned to see an old Plymouth coming up the hill. An elderly couple got out and slowly made their way over to where he was standing—in front of the workshop. The old man walked holding on to the woman's arm, not for support but for guidance. She smiled up at Jud and came to a stop. He walked slightly past her, then felt her hesitation and came to a halt as well.

"Hello," Jud greeted them. The lady nodded then looked to her man.

"Hello, back at ya," he said, looking in Jud's general direction with eyes clouded by age. "You the fella to see about takin' a fishin' trip?"

"I am."

"Well, I'm Fred Jones and this is my wife Ellen," whose smile broadened at the introduction. "And I want ya to take me on one of them float trips down the river. And I want to get started right away. 'Course," he laughed, "when you're seventy-five years old you want to get everything started right away." Then he laughed again, a short, giddy, slightly high-pitched laugh; sort of a chuckle gasping for air, somewhere between a hoot and a giggle; one part titter to two parts howl. Totally infectious.

Jud would never forget that laugh. It was a laugh that still made him smile every time he remembered it; a style of laughter you wouldn't expect from Fred—going by his looks. He was of medium height, moderate build, soft-spoken, and he dressed plainly. He was a mild man, unassuming. Like his last name, there was little to rescue Fred from the ordinary—save his signature laugh. It was funny by itself; it made everything else funny. It was tonic and elixir, a burst of helium in the everyday air.

A cabinetmaker all his life, Fred had been forced into retirement by his failing vision. He had come back that day to revisit another, sighted day from thirty-seven years earlier, a day he could now see in his mind more clearly than the day that lay before him. “It was a long time ago. I floated the river with Johnny Todd. He’s dead now. Did ya know him?”

“Sure, went to school with a lot of the Todd kids. There’s still quite a few Todds up and down the valley.”

“Well, we had a day of fishing that day, I’m tellin’ ya. And I want to do it again. We put the boat in the river right here in town, and floated down to a bridge. Do you know where I mean?”

“That would be Reynolds Bridge, about eight river miles from here,” Jud answered. “That’s the one.”

While they talked, Jud couldn’t help wondering just how this old man was going to fish, especially on the Elkheart, where the casting has to be done with pinpoint accuracy. But then Fred explained it to him.

“Got cataracts and they aren’t operable. So, I’m gradually going blind. But, right now I can make out shapes and colors. Can’t see anything in detail anymore. My whole world is kind of a watercolor, like I was lookin’ out a frosty window.

“Anyway, I figure if you get me pointin’ in the right direction, keep the boat at a steady distance from the bank, and you be my eyes, I’ll bet we could catch a few.

“Ellen can make a fine take-along supper. Lamb sandwiches, homemade bread, and apple pie. And we can bring along a couple of beers,” he winked. Fred had such a strong innocence to his face, it somehow exaggerated the simple drinking of a streamside beer to a near-felony. “So when can ya go?”

“Well,” Jud said as he looked at his pocket watch, “It’s three o’clock now.” Then he cogitated further, “Mmm, let’s get on the river around four o’clock. That way we should be floating over the best water at the best time.”

So it was agreed, and while Fred and Ellen drove down and checked into a room at the Take ’er Easy, Jud switched hats from boat builder to guide. He had backed the Willys up to the dory’s trailer and was bent over, hooking up the lights, looking up now and then to the mountains where the clouds had stopped merely forming and were now brewing, when suddenly he felt a strange and cool contraction in his flesh. Everyone knows the sensation: a sudden chill, the feeling of walking over somebody's grave, that you're-not-alone-in-an-empty-room sensation, the spooky kind of gooseflesh. At first he thought the feeling was barometric, but at the same time he was sensing, for some inexplicable reason, that things were going to be just right, strangely and irreversibly right. Everyone knows the feeling: when simple signs suddenly become omens, when you know that something is about to happen and that it's going to be good. The rarest of all premonitions—a positive one; when karma, intuition, and the elements collide; when all the forces come in to play and Edgar Cayce is blowing the whistle. Jud was having one of those premonitions.

As he slid the driftboat in at Town Bridge, there came the sound of distant thunder. The wind gusted. Jud was at the oars and Fred was in the bow. The *S.S. Lucky Me* drifted away from shore, heading into a certain storm. Jud shouted back to Ellen, who had opted to stay behind, dry and warm with her book back at the motel, "We'll be at Reynold's Bridge around nine o'clock, unless the north wind begins to blow; then you can look for us sometime next Thursday."

This made Fred laugh, which in turn made Jud laugh, as well as the two MacGregor boys who were fishing on the opposite bank. Why he was laughing, Jud hadn't a clue; it was black up ahead, and they were soon to be soaked. But he was hanging on to that premonition; it was strong, absolute, unmistakable—good things *were* in the wind. It just didn't look that way.

"Gonna rain, Jud," Rob MacGregor shouted.

Of course, Jud knew one more thing about his premonitions—sometimes they'd been wrong, real wrong.

The first few drops of rain hit them before they had floated a quarter mile. It was nothing more than a drizzle. But a mile later they were in the eye of the storm. The wind howled; the rain flew. Jud was rowing a man who was legally blind through a tempest, a man who could only identify colors and shapes. So, with the sky, water, and bank all muddied together into the edgeless grays of rainfall and low light, he was up against it as a guide.

The conditions were rough even for a sighted man, but Fred fished undaunted, the rain pouring off the brim of his hat, his line in a constant wrap, his fly stuck in everything but the water. He met every tangle with a joke or a laugh. The brightest color on board was the blue shining behind the gray of Fred's eyes. "Isn't this great?" Fred shouted over the wind. "Feel that air."

Trying to keep the boat straight with the current and every gust blowing him sideways, Jud was having a hard time sharing in the joy of it all—except when he heard Fred's laugh. Finally, the wind became so strong that Jud rowed the dory into a sheltered back eddy, deciding it was best just to sit and wait the wind out. Tying the boat off, he helped Fred through the deadfall until they were in a grove of birch trees, and out of the rain. They decided that then would be as good a time as any to have that first cold one.

As it turned out, the storm was as short lived as it was intense. In fact, they were seeing patches of blue returning to the sky upriver by the time they had finished their beers.

They fished on after devising a method: Jud tied a knot in Fred's line. He was to cast until he felt the knot in his hand, which would tell him that his cast had reached the distance needed, and it was time to slap his fly into the water and start stripping. He was using a big black streamer in deference to the brown trout; he was using ten-pound leaders in deference to the willows. Jud would then hold the dory a steady distance from the bank so that Fred's now-measured casts would land close to the willows but not in them. They hung up a few times, but no more than some of the sighted fishermen he had guided.

Fred was a good fisherman; Jud could tell by the relaxed and even way he handled his rod and line. But there was no avoiding the underwater snags, and Fred had just hung up his fly in another one. "Well, that feels like I just hooked another one of those big ones," Fred laughed. He broke the fly off and Jud tied another one on. Then he looked up to see Fred rummaging through his vest to produce a small camera. He snapped a picture of Jud without holding the camera to his eye, then he snapped a few more by just arbitrarily pointing the camera straight to the sky, downstream, upstream, east, and west.

"I'll bet that is some sky," he said, then he handed Jud the camera and asked, "How many pictures do I have left?"

The counter read thirty-four. Jud answered, "Two," and gave him back the camera.

"It's a no-brainer," Fred explained, "just a point-and-shoot. But it's just the ticket for me, anyway; if any of them are out of focus, I can't tell. When we get home our boy will bring the grandkids over for a slide show.

"Taking pictures of the whole vacation. Ellen and I are heading for the Grand Canyon tomorrow. It's where we spent our honeymoon, fifty-four years ago Saturday." Then he winked over a sly expression. "Gee, I hope she doesn't get any ideas."

The sun was making a comeback and within the hour was again shining on the riverscape. The river silvered in the pure light after a rain, the colors intensified, adding much more definition to Fred's vision, increasing his chances as an angler. They thought about the sandwiches but decided to fish on, to see what all this improved clarity and new light might bring. Jud began to feel the subtle stirrings of a realized premonition. The evening fishing on the Elkheart after a rain, a heavy rain, could be amazing.

And that evening, that old man and Jud had a time. The larger browns were out of their lairs and on the feed.

For the next two hours they had strikes, they had follows, they had misses, they had eleven fish on, and they landed four. The knot in the line was working. Jud would say, "Cast," and Fred would lay the fly pretty close to straight in.

It was when they were floating past where Stone Creek joined the river that Fred made a dead-on cast into the corner of a deep hole capped with river foam and covered by willows. Jud had no sooner said, "Good cast, Fred," that the foam bulged, the hole boiled, and the willows gave way to the surge of a brown trout, a most serious brown trout that hit Fred's fly going away. But instead of trying to return to his hole, the fish headed into the current. Fred's rod tip dove straight down, following the fish as it shot beneath the hull. They hit the confluence of Stone Creek with Fred's reel in full spin. Jud swung the boat to keep Fred's line free. But by the time he had the boat around, the line was spiraling down into the vortex of the melding currents, the rest of the line sweeping downstream. But despite the whirling boat, the swirling currents, and the spiraling line, Fred intuitively brought his rod tip back up and played the trout well.

"She's still on. I can feel her. I don't know where she is; hell, I don't know where I am, either. But she's still there and I want to tell you she's a dandy."

The line and Fred were soon straight to the fish. "We have a chance at her now," Jud shouted as he pushed hard against the oars to keep up with a brown trout that had a fifty-foot lead. Fred stood bandy-legged in the knee braces, his hands sure to his rod and reel, his laughter floating up and down the river.

The trout rolled to the surface, shaking and thrashing. A big fish. Four pounds or more. Then she rolled again.

She was at first the quarry, the mark, the game. Then she was the challenge, the opponent, the one to better. But with the second roll she went away the winner, the wiliest, a story to be told. Fred felt the slack in his line. The trout was gone.

Having been a guide for many years, Jud had seen the "big one getting away" scenario played out many times: Some swear, some experience instant depression, others shrug their shoulders and force a smile through pursed lips, then say something like "It's all part of the sport" or some such aphorism. At least he thought that's what they were saying, since it was sometimes hard to hear over the gnashing of their teeth.

But Fred met the loss with joyous recognition. He whooped and he hollered and he laughed. "How big was she? Did ya see her? I heard her."

"Twenty-two inches at the very least," Jud answered.

Reaching for his camera, he asked Jud to hold his hands twenty-two inches apart. Then pressing the shutter he said, "I'll call this picture 'The one that got away.'"

Jud remembered the evening ending in stories, lamb sandwiches, and pie. He'll always remember Fred fighting that fish. But, most of all, he'll remember the sound of Fred's laughter, and the spirit of an old man confronted with losing the most precious of our senses, sight; which has since kept the loss of a large trout perfectly clear through Jud's eyes.

There was Fred taking pictures of a landscape, for him dimmed and and imageless, save for the light of the moment and the colors of the day. There was Fred taking a picture of a fish he never saw so he could share the times he'd had, nearly blind, with someone sighted.

And there was Fred vibrant in the pleasures of simply being and living every sighted moment he had remaining to his seventy-five-year-old limit. He was going blind and doing so with an egoless dignity. He was still a fisherman in love with the art of the angle. He was life and he was lesson. He was amused by and agreeable to his time—past and present.

According to *Webster's Ninth New Collegiate Dictionary:* "**pas-time,** *n*, 15(c): something that amuses and serves to make time pass agreeably." Also see fly fishing.

8

~

Travels

*T*HE DETOUR OUT *of Missoula added seventy-seven unexpected miles to the road for Helena. There are very few highways in Montana, and being rerouted because of road closure, we left the concept of detour and entered into the world of adventure. The detour would have been pleasant under normal circumstances, even welcomed by Charley, who favors the slower speeds and the smells that come with a back road, but he was on edge, as was I—Rocinante had developed a slight hissing and knocking sound. Charley noticed the noise first, drawing my attention to it by the constant cocking of his head. It started as barely noticeable, but by the time we had hit Helena it had become a full-blown clatter.*

Along our way the detour took us through the small town of Travers Corners. There the Elkheart River runs through the Elkheart Valley following the glacial dictates of the Elkheart Range. It all lies within county lines: that would be Elkheart County. While the area might have suffered slightly from a certain lack of invention in the names—the views were extraordinary. I made an attempt to find a mechanic in Travers Corners, but the sign on the garage's door read, 'Gone to the Game.' Then I noticed the town seemed to be deserted. Everyone had gone to the game. I pushed on to Helena.

One good thing about the drive was that by some obscure reason, I was able to pick up the most wonderful radio station playing classical guitar—and the music fit the landscape. If I could trade whatever gifts I have been given in this lifetime for one thing—I would wish to be a musician.

This note, recently found in a basement in Helena, is one John Steinbeck wrote to himself. It was written on the back of a receipt from Wilson's Service, 134 Main Street. New fan belt and pulley—with labor—$14.95. The bill was dated October 14, 1960—the fall he traveled through Montana with Charley.

* * *

It wasn't one of those big mobile homes, nor was it particularly fancy. There was nothing to distinguish it, other than its being brand new, from any of the other trailer-and-winnebago types that roll through Travers Corners every fall—vacationers on their way home from Glacier, Canadians and retirees heading south for the winter. Unlike other motor homes, it bore no visual evidence of where it was going or where it had been. There were no decals, bumper stickers, or club emblems stuck to its side. There were no lawn chairs strapped on its back; no barbecue, no boat, no bicycles, no satellite dish, no awnings, none of the trailer-park trappings. It was generic and it was white. It was a rental.

Stopping at the flashing light, which swung on its wire in a very strong wind, the driver leaned out and asked directions of Flea Dodrill, who was walking in the crosswalk. "Jest go about a mile. Turn right at the first bridge ya see. The Boat Works is at the end of the road," Flea answered. The driver waved his thanks and motored north out of town.

He was called "Flea" not for some past infestation, nor was it because of his size, since Flea was a normal-sized rancher. He was Flea because as a boy in the backfield of the football team, he was "harder to catch than a flea in a cactus patch." At least that's what Coach Eaton said after Flea's final game. That game, like Flea's nickname, has never been forgotten around Travers Corners. Flea ran for four touchdowns, intercepted three passes, and pretty much single-handedly beat Gardiner for the town's first and only State Football Championship.

No longer moving like his namesake, Flea headed for McCracken's. He was moving slow. His back had gone out again. He was in the middle of haying, and haying needs all the back a man can give it. He needed Junior McCracken to fill a prescription. Pulling his hat down against the wind, he limped his way to the general store. The summer dust blew down Main Street. It was the end to another dry season.

Up at the Boat Works, it was impossible to hear the arrival of the motor home over the sound of the lathe. The driver was at the door, and his presence, suddenly noticed, gave Jud a slight start. He switched off the lathe. "Hello," he said, half shouting over the drone of the lathe, which was slowly winding down.

"I'm looking for Judson C. Clark."

"I'm Jud."

"A-a-ah, that's good, man, that's good. Can you take me fishing down the river tomorrow?"

"Well, I'd like to, but the river is too low to float."

Finding his way around two driftboats, one just finished and one under construction, the stranger stepped over a stack of cedar, tripping slightly on an extension cord, until he was closer to Jud at the lathe, which had wound down to a stop. The stranger was dressed in Levi's with a leather jacket over a T-shirt. His hair was long for his age. "I need, that's *need*, man, not want, man, but need, someone to show me where the good fishing is. You make these boats, man? They are gorgeous, like some kind of sculpture."

"Thanks," Jud answered.

The man was standing in the light near the windows, the piercing late-afternoon light of autumn. Creases fanned out from his eyes, which were tired and dark—hard and deep lines; the markings of a man who had lived life beyond its boundaries; the Mick Jagger lines of too much fun; the Johnny Cash lines of too much sorrow.

"My name is George Tickner," he introduced himself, shaking Jud's hand. Then over Jud's shoulder he spotted a guitar case. "You play the guitar?"

"Only when no one is around, or when someone I don't like is around. If I really don't like them—then I sing. I love music, unfortunately I have neither the time nor the talent to pursue it."

George laughed and rubbed the back of his neck. "That's a bummer, man. I mean about the river being low. I really dig floating along in the boat and fishing. But, okay, if the river is too low, maybe you can tell me someplace else to go. I am drivin' the mobile unit, man—I am portable. I want to go somewhere and hear nothing but the breezes. I am in need of some silence, man. I need to get away from people. Can you dig it? It's been a ridiculous three weeks, man." His voice was raw, used, with the rasp of cigarettes and whiskey—with musical and southern inflections, the vowel sounds getting an extra beat.

It took a lot more than just three weeks to get a face like that, Jud thought. "Do you play the guitar?"

"Only when *everybody* is listening," laughed George, "I . . ." A bark from the R.V. cut him short. "Hey man, would it be all right if I let my dog out? He's cool."

"No problem," Jud answered and looked around for Annie the Wonderlab, but she was presently out of the yard, up on the hill chasing mice, rabbits, whatever needed chasing. Not that there would be a problem if she had been around, for Annie, like most full-grown, eighty-pound labs, would acquiesce to a Pekinese. Labradors are not cowardly, but when confronted by violence they appear to rise above it, ignore it, not out of fear, but from intelligence.

George opened the R.V. and down the steps came a large black-and-brown dog, in no particular hurry. It looked like no other dog Jud had seen before; a tall dog, lanky, part deerhound maybe. It didn't merely walk across the yard to make a tree his own, he sort of slowly sauntered, moving like Miles Davis.

The dog then came over to sit beside George. His coat was long and curly, except for the hair between his long, drooping ears, where it was *very* long and curly, coiling into natural dreadlocks that hung down over his eyes. "This is my dog Bob Marley."

"So you're a musician?" Jud asked as he leaned over to pet Bob Marley, who was way too cool to dig attention.

"Yeah, I've been on the road, seventeen gigs in twenty-three days, brutal man, and I have to go back in four days and do another seventeen."

"What instrument do you play, Bob Marley?" Jud laughed at the dog's name, it being such a perfect match. Bob Marley answered in a groan, a Barry White, ultracool groan.

"Bob loves music, man. His job in the band is to keep time. Our sax player calls him the Mutt-ronome. Show Jud two-four time, Bob." Bob's tail wagged out a perfect two-four time. "Now do four-four time, Bob," George asked, reaching into his jacket for a piece of beef jerky. Bob's tail doubled its tempo in anticipation of his taste treat. "Very cool, Bob," and he tossed the dog his reward, "very cool, but you better be cool, man. You were named after the world's coolest dude." Bob groaned again.

"So, man, where am I going to go fishing if you can't float me?"

"Well, the river is too low to float, but it isn't too low to fish. I haven't been fishing in over a week myself, but Doc Higgins was in this morning and had a good day of fishing yesterday on the river."

"Okay, if I can't float . . ." George paused, then asked, "is there a place that some rancher might let me camp down on the river? I am totally self-contained, man. I wouldn't be a problem. Someplace quiet, man?"

"Mmmm . . . I don't know . . ."

"Where did this Doc Higgins fish, man?"

"He was out at the Dodrill Ranch."

"Would this Dodrill let me park someplace on his property? I'd be glad to pay him something for his trouble—in fact I would insist."

"Well, maybe . . ." Jud thought for a moment. He hated to call Flea and impose on his privacy, but he also knew that Flea had a small ranch and two kids in college, so, in a way, he hated to deprive him of the added income even more. . . . "I'll call him for you and see what he says."

"Hey, thanks, man, that's very kind."

The phone was busy the first time and in between tries he asked George about his music.

"I'm just part of a traveling lounge act, man."

"Flea? Yeah, this is Jud . . . yeah . . . good . . . How about you? Oh, no, again? No . . . No, I haven't, Flea, knock on wood, but I know it has to be painful . . . Hey, Flea, I gotta a guy standing here who has a mobile home and he's looking for a place to camp for a few days . . . Yeah . . . Yeah . . . You're kidding. That's funny . . . Yeah . . . Anyway, he wants to do a little fishing . . . Yeah . . . Yeah . . . And he wants to pay you something for it . . . Right . . . Okay . . . I'll tell him . . . Just a couple of days . . . Right . . . Okay . . . Hope your back is better soon . . . All right . . . Bye, Flea."

Hanging up the phone, Jud smiled at George. "You know the guy on the street a while ago who told you how to get up here?"

"Yeah?"

"That was Flea Dodrill. He was in town getting some pills."

"That is strange, man, but it's a good kind of strange. Some kind of providence there. Hey, Jud, if this guy's not feeling well, I mean, I don't want to bother the guy."

"No, it's his back. Goes out on him pretty often."

"Oh, man, I got a bad back. Some nights when I'm standing on stage for two hours, it goes out on me. It's the worst, man. The guitar, which doesn't weigh very much, turns into an anvil, man."

Jud followed George and Bob Marley back to the motor home, giving directions. "It's easy to find. Three miles out of town on the right. Mailbox says Dodrill. Turn there. The house sits down by the river."

"Is there a place where I could buy some flies and a few leaders?"

"McCracken's."

Stepping into the van for a moment, George was quickly back out with a stack of cassette tapes. "A guy I know is in the music business. He's like forever sending me promo tapes. Here," and he handed Jud the cassettes, "I don't know what all is in there, but it's bound to have a few of the biggies. And, thanks, man, I mean I really appreciate it."

"Well, thanks, and I hope you have good fishing."

"Yeah, and some real good quiet as well, man."

Flea and his wife Polly came out to meet the motor home as it rolled up to the ranch house. Bob Marley, riding shotgun, was all nose—barnyard smells. He was wagging in three-quarter time. After the introductions and small talk, and after a particularly loud and extra-cool groan from Bob as he caught the scent of the river, George was the first to speak. "That was pretty amazing, man, you being the guy I asked directions from this morning."

"Small town in a small world," Flea replied, smiling, slightly bent with back pain.

"How's the back doing?" George asked.

"Better than a train wreck, maybe. Got the hay all down and now I gotta put on an extra hand to bale it up."

Thinking the reference to money was Flea's country opening for negotiations, George replied, "I sure do appreciate you letting me camp here, man, and I insist on paying you something for your trouble."

"Can't charge a fella for something he ain't done yet. So you go ahead have yer vacation, and when ya leave, just stop by and leave what ya think's right in the mail box."

"That sounds more than fair."

So the bargain was struck. Flea told him the best campsite on the river, and pointed the way down. Polly added, "And if you need anything, just give a holler."

"Well, that's very kind. You know, Flea, that's the second time today you've given me directions. Maybe now you can tell me where I might find the best fishing?"

"Hard tellin' for sure, but I'd say my first choice would be the river." George laughed and Flea and Polly laughed with him. Bob groaned. "Oh, this is my dog, Bob Marley. He's cool. He doesn't chase cows, he doesn't chase rabbits, he doesn't chase anything. Bob is definitely too cool to run. He'll just hang around camp, pick a spot where the vibrations are good, and groove there all day long."

"That's all right," Flea answered, "the cattle are all up in the hills, anyways. Have a good time."

Polly and Flea turned back to the ranch house as George aimed the mobile unit toward the river. "Feller talks funny, but I kinda liked him," Flea said, scratching his head.

"He's got a kind face," Polly said. "But what kind of a name is Bob Marley for a dog?"

The next several days were heaven on earth for George and Bob. George would go to sleep when the night fell, and arise when he felt like it. The first morning he slept until noon. His hours revolved around fishing, cooking, and relaxing in a folding chair overlooking the river. The grove of cottonwoods secreted him from the rest of the world. He didn't read anything. He didn't listen to a radio. His only conversations were with Bob. He didn't go to town. Once in a while he would hear the drone of Flea's baler in the distant fields. Every other sound was muted by the murmur of the river.

The fishing was slow, but it felt marvelous—he'd caught a few. The cooking was great as he made the dishes his mama made when he was a boy in the hills of Tennessee. And kicking back on the banks of the Elkheart River in the quiet was so sweet and easy. The nights were cool and the days were calm.

Bob Marley, who was getting along in years—there were shades of gray showing in his dreadlocks—just picked a shady spot and grooved each day, listening to the river rhythms, the breeze in the trees—the original woodwinds.

The sound of an old Ford tractor came through the cottonwoods and willows. Bob Marley heard it first. He cocked his head and made a curious groan. But George knew the sound. He knew the parts that made that sound. His old man had had that same kind of tractor, and most of his boyhood was spent riding on or wrenching on that damned old thing. He didn't smile when he thought about it. Flea came chugging into camp.

"Hello there, Flea," George greeted him.

"Polly and I ain't seen hide nor hair of ya since ya came down here. She began pesterin' me to go and see if everything was all right. I says the man's fishin'—of course he's all right."

"Flea, there is nothing on God's green earth that could make this place any better."

On Flea's lap balanced a plate covered with a cloth napkin. He killed the tractor, climbed down, and handed the dish to George. "Polly thought you might like some of her homemade biscuits."

"God, they look just like the ones my mama used to make. Well, that's very kind of Polly." The biscuits were still warm and George hurriedly took them inside and brought them out sliced and buttered. Offering Flea one and motioning to the cooler sitting in the shade, he asked, "Have some cold drinks in there—ice tea or beer?"

"Thanks," Flea said, grabbing a beer; then he asked, "So, how's the fishin'?"

"Well, I've caught a few, but they ain't exactly jumping onto the hook, man. But the fishing, man, like everything else about this place, is just so fine." George stepped back, to look first up and then down the river. "Not a sound nor a soul in sight. It's Shangri-la, man. Bob and I have been enjoying ourselves to the maximum. How about a little bite of homemade biscuit, Bob?" Bob Marley groaned and beat out a four-four time, raising small clouds of dust as he wagged the downbeat. "You and Polly are lucky, man. I could really dig living here."

"Yeah, I suppose we are, but ever' once't in a while, Polly and me sure would like t' git away from this place. Git ourselves one of them R.V.s, and jest go. No place partic'lar in mind, jest go. Jest motor ourselves south, idling from one warm spot to the next." Flea's eyes closed briefly just thinking about it. "This wish gits extra-strong durin' calvin' season when it's ten degrees and there's a thirty-mile-an-hour wind ablowin'," Flea laughed.

"Judging by the way you got down from the tractor, I'd guess your back isn't doing any better?"

"Hell, no. It goes out at least twice a year. Been to Doc Higgins, been sent to specialists. Been to the Gyro-quacktors. Polly even took me to one of them acupuncturists. Got myself punctured, didn't do a goddamned thing. There ain't nothin' seems to work."

"I got a bad back, too, man, and sometimes it goes out. Way too painful, man."

"What do you do?"

"I have some pills."

"Damn pills ain't worth nothin'. All they do is make ya logy and in the mornin' the pain's there waitin' fer ya."

"God, these biscuits are good," George said. "Tell Polly many thanks."

"Polly headed up to Reynolds to see her mom—won't be back until late."

"Flea, I made one hellacious chili this morning—been simmering all day long. Why don't you join me for supper, man?"

"Well. . . . I guess . . . sure I will, but I gotta couple more hours ahead of me, yet. Gotta check on that Jenkins boy who's running the baler. Seventeen years old. Needs watching. Then I gotta get some water moved. Be back around eight." He climbed up on the tractor, giving a moan as he did. He turned the key and the Ford whined but didn't start. "C'mon girl." Flea smiled. "Sometimes you have to sweet-talk these old gals to git 'em started."

"I remember."

"You know about these old Fords?"

"I was raised on a farm in Tennessee. And, yessir, I know something about these old Fords."

The tractor finally kicked over and Flea chugged his way back through the trees. When George first asked him to stay for dinner, Flea wasn't too sure about it. He felt a little uneasy around George; maybe it was the way he talked. I mean the guy was definitely different. He could sense it. But, when he knew about Ford tractors, Flea thought he might be okay. He wondered what the guy did for a living, then he wondered why his baler had stopped dead in the far field.

A few hours later, Flea came back to the campsite, this time driving his pickup, his hair still wet from a shower. The twine disc on the baler had broken. He was an hour in the truck back and forth to Reynolds for the new parts. If his back was hurting before, it was killing him now. He'd tossed down a few more muscle relaxers. They were beginning to help—a little. It would be twenty-nine years this October that he'd had a trick back.

With his feet up on the cooler and tilted back in his lounge chair, George sat facing the river. He was unaware of Flea's arrival. He was holding a guitar. But as Flea was about to say hello, the music started.

At first he played the beginnings of familiar songs. Flea would be just remembering one and then came another. One famous tune after another. Then George shifted in his seat and held the guitar closer. "Malagueña," then "El Condor Pasa" stirred the evening air; the resonance of a twelve-string floated over the river, echoing off the water, to echo once more against a thick stand of birch on the other shore. The music—whole bass notes over four-string finger picking, the bar chords over untroubled waters—was beautiful. The acoustics amazing. So beautiful, Flea could hardly do anything else but sit down.

It was only when the song had ended that George noticed Flea sitting on a stump, more biscuits on his lap and a six-pack of beer at his feet. "Well, I never, and I don't think I'd be lyin'—I never heard anything that pretty in my entire life."

"Well, thanks, Flea. How long you been sitting there?"

"Long enough to know that you've played that guitar more'n once."

"Yeah, it pays the bills." George smiled as he stood. He leaned the guitar carefully against his chair and unfolded another one for Flea. "C'mon over and sit down. Put that back of yours in a chair, man."

"I was wondering what ya did. Golly, that sure is a pretty thing," Flea said of the guitar as he eased down in his chair.

"Yeah, it was a gift."

The chili was served, a few cold ones were cracked, Bob Marley mooched a few more biscuits, and they spent the evening talking of their lives. Ford tractors. Farm life. Ranch life. The same life. Nearly the same age, both from large families, George's life closely paralleled Flea's in many ways—until they reached eighteen. Flea stayed on the ranch, while George took his guitar, thirty-seven dollars, and, he explained, "I left that farm and never looked back. My old man was a mean-spirited, Baptist, child-beating son-of-a-bitch. My mama was a saint. I stayed to finish high school, just for her, then I was gone. Things were lean for years, man. I had more guitar to learn and a lot of other things to learn. Nashville was a long way from Boone County." George laughed. "Hey, how'd you get the name 'Flea'?"

Flea then told him about the State Championship, the football game, his place in Elkheart County pigskin history, about Coach Eaton saying he was as hard to catch as his nickname, about the winning touchdown. "It was on that last touchdown that this kid from Gardiner, who was about two hunnnert and fifty pounds, but slower than molasses—I'd been runnin' around him for the whole game—decided to git his revenge. He was in on the last tackle and he came down on me hard. My back hurt some then, and has just gotten worse over the years. Now every year it goes out at least twice. Doc Higgins said I could git it operated on, but I never liked the idea. I . . ." He was interrupted by a flashlight and the sound of someone coming up the path. It was Polly. George stood as she entered the camp.

"Hi there, Polly," Flea greeted, a little surprised to see her.

"Hello, George," she said kindly, then quickly turned to Flea. "Do you know what time it is, Flea Dodrill?"

Not wearing a watch, Flea said, "Well, no, I don't," kind of wincing—wincing from a twitch in his back; and wincing from the tone in his wife's voice.

"George," Polly was one to come to the point, "with his back out lately, Flea, here, has been a little owly, but when you add tired, which he's gonna be tomorrow, then you have one real grumpy Flea on your hands."

"Yer right, yer right," Flea agreed. "I am sorry. I had no idea it had gotten that late—honest. But George and me, well, we got a lot in common." Polly raised one eyebrow.

"We were born the same year, both of us raised on a farm. Both from big families. So, one story just kinda kept leading to another. And, Polly, well, come over here fer a minute, will ya?" Flea had a silly grin on his face.

She walked over, counting the beer bottles as she went. "Flea Dodrill, you're drunk."

"No I ain't, Polly, I've had three beers all night, promise." Polly shot a look at George.

"God's truth," George nodded.

"Now please sit down, here." George took his guitar off the chair and Flea pulled the chair closer.

"Flea, now we really should get back," she said, sitting down.

"Polly, I know I've been a bit of a rattlesnake lately, and I apologize. I promise I won't be grumpy tomorrow. But I want ya t' sit right here. Just fer a little while. You jest have to listen t' this. George, could you play a song for Polly?"

"Be glad to, Flea."

"What's your favorite song, Polly?" George asked.

"Well, gosh, I don't know."

"Okay, what are some of your favorite songs?"

"You always liked ones by Patsy Cline," Flea volunteered.

George began tuning his guitar. "The night air has done some strange things to my strings, man."

Flea just sat and smiled at Polly until she became a little embarrassed and uncomfortable. She was feeling a little sheepish at the way she came in and sort of snapped Flea's head off in front of George. She laughed inwardly at the thought of Flea and this man having *anything* in common.

Bob Marley sauntered over to where Flea was sitting and nuzzled his hand. George was surprised. "Bob—ordinarily—doesn't like strangers."

"Despite my name, dogs have always taken a likin' t' me."

Then a dozen strings, echoing all through the woods and over the river—"Crazy," "I Go Out Walking After Midnight"—twelve strings became a band of guitars. Polly was amazed and delighted. "The sound is so incredible!" Then George played the blues and took his Gibson for a "Walk on the Wild Side."

"A little river-reverb there, Bob Marley. Very cool. Show 'em three quarter-time, man. Very cool," George said as he strummed the final chord. Bob drummed out the beat.

"Isn't that about the purtiest thing you ever did hear?" Flea asked. Polly agreed, "It was so beautiful." A tear came to her eye. She and Flea were holding hands.

"He plays music for a livin', Polly."

"Small wonder."

"He's been practically every place twice. Travels all the time."

"Yeah, in fact I'll be leaving tomorrow morning. Not too early but early enough. I catch a flight out of Helena and then on to New York."

"Do you play with any band we ever heard of?" Polly asked.

"Not a chance. We're just about a bunch of hackers in a glorified lounge act."

"Well, I never heard anyone play the guitar like that before." Polly yawned. "Flea, we had better get on home."

"Doggone it. I wish it was suppertime again. I'd like to relive this night all over," Flea said, slowly getting up. "We'll see you in the morning. We'll be out in the far field. We'll give you a wave."

"And ya know what we said about payin' us somethin' fer yer stay, well fergit it. T' see that tear come t' Polly's eye, and t' hear that music, out here on our river, well that's payment enough, I reckon." His arm was fully around her waist. She was a little surprised, as Flea wasn't one for showing affection in front of other people, or to speak of it, either.

"Many thanks, Flea."

"You come back any old time. You take care. See ya, Bob Marley." Bob groaned as Flea gave him a few pats on the head.

Polly stopped just as she was about to get in the pickup. "Have ya had any luck with yer fishin'?" Polly asked.

"Not too much."

"When Doc Higgins comes out, he spends most of his time fishing down where the river splits."

"Thanks, I'll give that a try."

On the ride back to the house, Flea sat smiling. "You sure look happy for someone with a bad back," Polly wondered. "You sure you didn't have more than just a few beers?"

"Well, about an hour ago, I took a pill that George's doctor gives him when his back goes out."

"Flea, you shouldn't'a done that . . . you had those beers. Ya darned old fool. You could have yourself an adverse reaction. You shouldn't be taking another man's medicine."

"Three beers in three hours ain't drinking, Polly," he said, taking her hand again. "Anyways, I had to try somethin' else. The back's worse this time than ever. I sure am gettin' tired, Polly. George said I would. But you know, my back seems to be feelin' better. I love you very much."

Now Polly was concerned, and slid across the seat to ride close to him just like she did the night Flea won the State Championship.

So, it was one last try for the trout. George was up before sunup and had walked two bends down river by dawn. By the time he had reached the place where the river splits, sunlight was full on the water. The river was wide and shallow and barely moving before falling by riffles into the two channels. The mountains and the cottonwoods reflected a mirror-perfect image in the quiet water; then, as the current increased, tumbling around the tip of an island, the images became lineless until the colors ran with the river.

One channel was receiving most of the water, while the other one was small and heavily wooded, like a creek unto its own. He had time to fish only one of them. He chose the smaller one. It was more like the ones he fished as boy in the foothills of the Smokies.

The mosquitoes were still. There wasn't a breath of moving air. George followed a path paralleling the stream as it tumbled through a stand of birch trees, cascading over deadfall and a beaver dam. Light filtered through the trees. It was the earliest he'd been up in years. He thought about Flea and Polly. How different their lives were from his. He'd led their kind of life and escaped it at first chance; and now after thirty years on the road, he envied it.

Many of his fishing skills were rusty, at best, as he seldom had a chance to use them. His tackle was the best money could buy. His knowledge of the sport was limited. When it came to hatches, genus and species were not factors. If the flies on the water were little white ones, then that's what he would take from his box. He only fished dry flies. Knots didn't come quickly.

But his casting was good, casting being timing, and timing being everything to a musician.

Slipping into the water, well behind the beaver damn, he looked behind him to a mangle of willows and deadfall. Backcast hell. No room for error. Long casts were going to be difficult, but necessary. There were no fish feeding. He chose a fly from his box, one that he particularly liked. He couldn't think of the name of it as he fumbled with his glasses to tie it on.

He angled himself in the trees and delivered a cast that threaded its way through branch and limb to land perfectly, if not a little miraculously, precisely where he wanted it to. A fish took the second it landed. Totally unprepared and still, perhaps, a little sleepy, he missed the fish—and a good-sized trout at that.

Now he was awake.

He tried another cast, this time landing the fly closer to the dam, in the foaming bubbles trailing off the branches of the beaver's work. Another fish took and was on only for a moment—a jump—then was off and gone.

He fished from one small pool to the next, each pool holding fish; and he was catching them, landing as many as he was missing. Good-sized fish all of them, the biggest about sixteen inches. He was having the morning of his angling life. Brown trout and beautiful.

By the time he was once again standing at the tip of the island, more time had slipped away than he had counted on. All he could think about was what kind of trout lurked in the other channel; but there was not time left to find out. He could see the mobile home parked upriver among the trees and Bob Marley curled up on the bank, asleep in the midmorning sun. He had to leave, and looking at his watch, he knew he needed to leave soon. Walking up the shallows back to camp, George was making casts; casts that had held neither design nor intention, mindless casts made without promise, made for no other purpose than to watch his fly float upon the water. His eyes glazed over with a daydream, his fly bobbing along in the riffles, well out of focus, as he watched the sky and the river go by. Images from his life flashed in his mind: musical moments, the insane concerts, the frenzied crowds, the hard partying, his two boys, one in college, one in rehab, his two ex-wives, the hellacious life on the road, his boyhood home in Tennessee.

So, when the fish sipped down his fly, he paid no attention to it. The trout spit the fly only to hook itself again, by chance, in the corner of its mouth. It was only when the current took up the slack that the rainbow, a full-sized rainbow, was aware of the hook and, in accordance with nature, took flight. The trout came as a complete surprise and nearly jerked the rod from George's hand. The fish jumped. She was enormous. Traveling at a great speed, the rainbow swept an arc across the river, and jumped again. Then she took off fast, heading for the channels. George took off after her. His line was now into the backing. He tried to run, nearly falling on the slippery bottom. He hadn't run in years. His heart was pounding. The rainbow made for the channel with the most water. He saw her wake as she made for the current, her silver coming through the curl. His line went limp. She was free.

Sitting on a bank to catch his breath, George was at first saddened at losing such a prize. He then marveled at the size, the strength, and the beauty of that fish. Jumping twice, she'd afforded him a good look at her. The moment was electric. If the rainbow had been music, she would have been an Eric Clapton riff, a drum roll by Ginger Baker, a scream of Otis Redding's. She would have been Little Richard at the wheel of a hotrod Lincoln. Or Jerry Lee jumping free. She was flat-out rock and roll.

If only the music could still give him the kick that trout just did. He looked at his watch. He had to go.

With Bob Marley riding shotgun—Bob preferred to think of himself as a sideman—George drove the mobile unit from the river. As he left the ranch house heading for the highway, he could see Polly and Flea in a distant field. They were quite a distance, but it looked as though Flea was doing jumping jacks. George got out the binoculars. He *was* doing jumping jacks. George was too far away to hear him laughing and *ya-hooing*.

It was a miracle as far as Flea was concerned. His back felt better than it had in years. He'd slept like a rock. He knew it could go out again, but for right now he wasn't just feeling better, he was feeling fine.

Polly had hardly slept a wink with worry. Flea's sleep was so sound, so deep. All night she checked on him. Flea, usually a tosser and turner, never moved a muscle. He never stopped smiling, and while he didn't talk in his sleep, he did laugh. His dreams, though he couldn't remember but one the next morning, had been vivid. "Polly, all night it was like I was floatin' in warm water. Like I was in Hawaii or somewhere. Tropical fish everywhere. And while I was floatin', mermaids were swimmin' beneath me, and rubbin' my back. All around people were laughin' and dancin', and havin' a good time. And all the time, you were right there with me."

"You old fibber, you. What would you want someone like me for in a dream full of mermaids?"

"'Cause I love you."

Blushing at the sincerity of Flea's tone, Polly responded, "One thing for sure—you been full of the sweet talk since George gave you that pill."

"Yeah, and tonight I am taking you into Reynolds for dinner, and then I wanna come home, and then I wanna . . ."

Wheeling the motor home up to Highway 43, stopping for a moment to deposit a note in the Dodrill mailbox, George drove toward Helena. "Looks like the pill did Flea some good," he said to Bob Marley. He was both glad and relieved to see that it had. After he had given it to Flea, he'd had second thoughts, for the pill was strong, effective, and at times intense, but not exactly approved by the FDA.

A musician since the '60s, George had seen all the drug and alcohol abuse he wanted to see over the years—through his own addictions and through those around him. Now, for a good time, he might drink a few beers, but that's as far as he takes it. Except for when his back goes out; then he goes straight for a prescription to Dr. Felonious B. Feelgood, druggist to the stars, and longtime personal physician to Elvis.

The note George left, wrapped around four crisp one hundred dollar bills, read:

"Dear Flea and Polly,

"You might think the money extravagant, but realize two things—the lousiest hotel in New York City costs one hundred dollars a night, and staying with you was better than the Plaza.

"Flea, I know you fantasize about being on the road, man—so save this money—think of it as a little gas cash from me to you. Drive Polly somewhere warm this winter. It'll do you good. Me, if given the chance, man, I would buy a place just like yours and never go anywhere again.

"The fishing this morning, well, you wouldn't believe it. It was great. I even have a "one that got away" story.

"If I were a songwriter and not a musician, I'd write a song about the

Elkheart River and your kind hospitality. But I'm not, so just know that you two and your wonderful ranch will be in my thoughts when I'm on the road—sharing my travels with Bob Marley."

* * *

(*Author's note:* The guitar in the story, the Gibson given to George as a gift, was given by Leo Kottke—a thank you for helping him with an album. As for all those tapes given to Jud back at the Boat Works—if one were to read the liner notes, he would see George Tickner's name playing backup for the likes of Doctor John, Paul Simon, and Ry Cooder. The glorified lounge act he was leaving the Elkheart to rejoin was Bonnie Raitt and her band.)

So, now, perhaps, the reader can see the connection, that common bond, that formed so quickly between George and Flea. The connection Polly couldn't see at all. They were both famous. Flea famous in his world, George famous in his—the only difference being that George's world was slightly more global—a difference not noticeable from the banks of a river.

9

~

D. Downey

FROM THE DIARY of Traver Clark, September 17th, 1873:

We are heading into the country far north of the Yellowstone. It is uncommonly wild ahead, says our guide, Albie, a man with but one name—no first name, no last name, just Albie. He says much of the country we will be seeing has been seen by only a few white men. Mostly uncharted; in fact, unnamed.

I ride a horse that Albie has neglected to name, and trod along day to day behind D. Downey, who has but an initial for a first name. He will never divulge what the D. stands for, and he has sworn his sister Carrie to secrecy as well.

So I ride a horse with no name, into a part of the territory which has yet to be named, behind a man who has only a partial name, and led by a guide with only one name. The whole idea of it—well, it isn't frightening, but it is, admittedly, a little disconcerting—and at the same time marvelously exhilarating.

Albie has heard from the fur traders that there are cutthroat trout as long as your arm where we are headed.

* * *

So far it has been Tuesday as usual around Travers Corners, an average late-August day, maybe a little warmer than most. Other than a few parked cars around town, a couple in front of McCracken's, a couple over at the bank, the only signs of life have been a big black dog asleep across the double yellow line on Main Street, and Ed's son, Pete, shooting baskets down at the Chevron station. Pete's been tending the station, since Ed has gone to Reynolds for parts.

Despite his five-foot-eleven stature, Pete moved like a seven-footer. He was the high school's MVP and he was All Conference last year, regarded as the best basketball player in the Elkheart Valley. He was cool and he was cocky about it. His uniform accented his fluidity: baseball cap on backward, shirt unbuttoned and sleeves missing, a red oil rag hanging from the hip pocket of his Wranglers, which were one part denim to two parts grease.

He was dribbling, contemplating either a layup with the imaginary hang time of Doctor J., or a thirty-foot set shot with the fingertip roll of Larry Bird. "Pistol Pete," they call him. He was a natural to earn the name. He can dribble behind his back, between his legs, between the legs of his opponents; and he was suspended for one game last season for dribbling through a cheerleader's legs. But, when a dark green Bentley pulled up to the pumps, tripping the attendant's bell, Pistol Pete dribbled one into his knee. He'd never seen a car like this. The ball slammed off the Coke machine, bounced into an oil stain, then through a puddle of rusty radiator water, and into the opening door of the Bentley.

A man stepped from the car. A thick-bodied man with a mane of red hair that was windblown and streaked with gray. His dress was fastidious despite obvious travel: tan slacks, barely wrinkled, white shirt without a crease. Frowning, the man leaned over and inspected the door of his car, then shook his head and inspected Pete. The Pistol had misfired, a self-inflicted wound to his own coolness; and all that could be heard was a slight hissing sound of Pete's fluidity draining from his body, leaving nothing but an apologetic and gawking teenager.

"Gee, I'm sorry Mister, I . . ."

"Yes, I am sure that you are. Tell me something, young man. Is this the only service garage in town?"

"Yep."

"Might I speak to the owner?"

"Nope."

"And why would that be?"

" 'Cause the owner's my dad and he's gone up to Reynolds."

"Will he be back soon?"

"Nope."

"I trust that he will be back someday?" An irritation, not lost on Pete, grew in the man's voice. Pete was usually glib with locals and tourists alike, but this guy wasn't a tourist; he was a foreigner, and the distinction made Pete uneasy.

"What is your name, young man?"

"Pete."

"Peter is a fine name. My brother's name. Tell me something, Peter, would you happen to know a man by the name of Judson C. Clark?"

"Sure."

"Do you know where he might be found?"

"You bet."

"Would you care to share your knowledge with me?" The irritability was gone from the stranger's voice as it was obvious the boy was trying to help, as evidenced by the fact that he had started cleaning the Bentley's door. Pete was obviously bright with the keen eyes of a point guard, but the man found his one-word answers annoying; but the English will never understand brevity, while in Montana brevity is the chosen language.

"Jud lives here in town," Pete answered as he used his shirttail to bring a better shine to the door. "Lives up at the Boat Works. That's his place you see up there on the hill." Pete stood and pointed it out. "All you can see is the roof line. You just go outta town about a half-mile and there is a dirt road that angles back on the right. Cross the bridge. Go up the hill and the Boat Works is at the end."

"Would you know, by any chance, if he is any relation to your town's founding father, Traver C. Clark?"

"You bet. Traver was Jud's great-grandfather."

The stranger beamed. "Splendid! That is simply splendid."

"Could you tell me which of these peaks is Mt. D. Downey?"

"The biggest one you see, straight over the roof of the Tin Cup," Pistol said, pointing. "Is that a Rolls Royce, Mister?"

"It's a Bentley, and I have brought it from England at great expense. My name is Sir Gordon Pendelton, Peter, and I plan to be in your area for over a month," he said, reaching into the car for a neatly folded tweed jacket from which he pulled a crisp twenty-dollar bill. Handing it to Pete, he continued, "I will want you to take special care of the old girl while I am here. I want you to look at this money not as a tip, young man, but as a bribe. The Bentley is thirty-seven years old and she requires a great deal of care, so I will pay you now to make sure that she gets your very special attention."

"You bet."

"Right now you may fill her with your leaded gasoline. Tomorrow, I will want you to give her a thorough cleaning, change her oil, and tend to all her vitals. I will give you complete instructions on how I will want this done. Now, where might I purchase some scotch whiskey?"

"Right across the street at McCracken's."

"Thank you very much. I will be right back. Clean the windows, won't you, Peter? That's a good chap."

The Pistol was back. He was twenty dollars richer and he hadn't done a thing.

He tended to the Bentley, first the gas, then the windows, and he marveled at the car. The lines, the chrome, the lady on the hood ornament, the grill, the running boards, the interiors of leather and wood. It was so big. Like a limo from the movies. The Bentley was a far cry from the usual cars that pulled up to the Chevron. Nothing like this had ever pulled up to his dad's pumps before and the Bentley began to draw a crowd. The two Harris boys pulled up on their bikes, and from across the street, out of the Tin Cup Bar, came Vernon, who had spotted the Bentley from his personal stool at the rail. Vernon's a nosy old cowboy, one of the worst gossips in town; not the worst in the malicious sense of the word, just the worst because his hearing suffers from age, Ancient Age, and he gets things a little backward.

When Sir Gordon came through the door of the general store, Junior McCracken was busy, too busy to look up. Mary and Sally had both phoned in sick this morning and all day Junior had been running the checkout and the pharmacy. Doing two things at once was not Junior's forte. There was some sort of flu bug in town and he was filling his twelfth prescription since noon. He was on the phone with Doc Higgins taking another. "Right, Doc . . . Okay . . . Yeah . . . Busier than a bird dog. Bye." Junior hung up only to have the phone ring again instantly.

Even Sir Gordon, who had never seen Junior before, could tell that this was a harried and distracted man. Normally Junior is tightly wound, but today he looked like he might unravel. He was back and forth behind the counter of the pharmacy, pacing to the length of the phone cord and back again. Sir Gordon found his bottle of scotch, but not without some looking, since McCracken's is a big store carrying at least one each of everything, and to shop there, one needs to adjust to Junior's approach to the world of merchandising. Sir Gordon found the liquor department, or most of the liquor department, sandwiched in between the toiletries and baling twine. If Sir Gordon had been a gin drinker, he would have found his intoxicant on the opposite side of the store, on the same shelving as the irrigation boots and canned goods. He went to the front counter and waited for Junior to notice him and get off the phone.

"Half the town is down with it. Kids mostly, but Mary and Sally managed to catch it. Doc Higgins says it looks to be a twenty-four-hour thing." Junior then saw the stranger waiting by the register. "Gotta run. I'll have it ready for you in an hour." As soon as Junior was off the phone, he was out of the pharmacy section and almost running down the center aisle where the shopper could find apples, oranges, motor oil, horseshoe nails, batteries, stove pipe, kerosene, candy, and magazines.

"Sorry, I didn't see you standing there. Got a flu bug going around town. Been busier than a bird dog." Reaching for the bottle of scotch to read the price, Junior asked, "Will this be all?"

"Quite right. If I could trouble you for a little information? Might you know one Judson C. Clark?"

"Sure do."

"Then might you know if this would be a scotch he would like?"

"I think it might be very difficult to find a scotch Jud didn't like. In fact, he'll drink about anything he doesn't have to pay for." Junior laughed at his own joke, explaining, "Jud's an old friend of mine. Where are you from?"

"Henley-on-Thames, which is two hours west of London."

"What brings you to Travers Corners?"

Sir Gordon picked up his scotch and started for the door. Knowing that the reasons for his coming were a long and complicated story, he answered simply, "I've come to do a little fishing."

Junior wanted to talk more about fishing, as he always wanted to, but before he could say another word the phone began to ring in the pharmacy.

"Thank you so much," Sir Gordon said and was out the door and on his walk back to the gas station. He was crossing the street just as Pete was telling Vernon, while the two Harris boys still on their bikes listened in, all of what he knew about the car and its driver.

"His name is Sir Gordon Pendelton, or something like that, and he shipped his car; it's a Bentley; ain't it something? Looks like a Rolls Royce, huh? Anyways, he ships this car over from England just so he can have it over here to drive around in. The reason he's here is to see Jud. Being a Sir, that's kinda like being a duke or an earl or something, ain't it?"

Vernon wasn't sure.

"Check it out, Vern. He gives me this twenty-dollar bill and wants me to take real good care of his car while he's here. A twenty and I hadn't done a thing!" Then Pistol saw Sir Gordon coming and got busy polishing the hood ornament. Vernon headed back to the bar with the news: A duke or something was in town to see Jud. The Harris boys took off pedaling and once they were home, they would report to their mother about some king from another country that was handing out twenty-dollar bills down at the service station.

Inspecting the windows, Sir Gordon said, "Splendid. Many thanks for doing that. I have never seen so many insects, on any of my travels, as you have here in Montana. And your grasshoppers, they do make such a ghastly display of themselves when they hit. Tomorrow I will need to have her washed—mild soap, warm water. But I will go over all that with you—and your father?"

"He'll be here."

Then Sir Gordon repeated the directions to the Boat Works as he opened the door to the classic old car: "Out of town one half mile, then back to the right and up the hill?"

"Yep." Pete watched Sir Gordon wheel the Bentley out onto Main and he thought about the twenty, thinking if he made that kind of money for doing the windows, what would he make for doing the whole car? Pete imagined a chain of car washes, his own Bentley. The Pistol was so hot he was smoking. He picked up the ball and threw it against the garage, then took the bounce off the wall as he would an inbound pass; he faked left, he faked right; he did his own announcing: "The clock's winding down. Only five seconds to go. It's all up to the Pistol." He dribbled past the tire rack, then stopped and pulled up short of the diesel pump for a three-point jumper. "Nothing but net."

Sir Gordon turned right, crossed the wooden bridge spanning Carrie Creek, then angled sharply up the hill—an angle too steep for the long and low Bentley, and her back bumper scraped. The grinding noise made him wince, and patting the steering wheel, he apologized. "Sorry about that, old girl."

As he crested the hill, the old carriage house came into view and the sign out front he read aloud, "CARRIE CREEK BOAT WORKS AND GUIDE SERVICE, JUDSON C. CLARK, PROPRIETOR. Splendid." He smiled the smile and sighed the sigh of a man who had reached his destination. It had been three thousand miles by ocean liner, and two thousand miles by Bentley. But here he was in the Elkheart Valley, and the view from the Boat Works was spectacular.

He parked at the end of a row of driftboats, in the shade of some aspens. Grabbing first a magazine, then an old fly-rod case, the scotch, and finally a rather large briefcase, he followed the sounds of hammering and Jerry Garcia.

A large dog came wagging up to greet him, a very large dog, one that could be part Newfoundland: the country, not the breed. He nuzzled into Sir Gordon's lightly colored trousers, leaving a substantial amount of drool and dark hair. Sir Gordon tried to shoo the animal away, but with his arms full, the shooing gesture was mistaken for attempts to play that caused the dog to jump, nuzzle, shed, and drool all the more.

The Grateful Dead were getting closer. Sir Gordon rounded the corner of the old carriage house to see an open shed and workshop in the rear. A river dory was suspended by block and tackle and hung upside down in the middle of the shed. Beneath it he could see the bottom half of a man.

"Hello." Sir Gordon called as the dog jumped, attempting to grab the rod case in his teeth, hoping for a game of tug-of-war.

"Hello back."

"I am looking for a Mister Judson C. Clark."

"That's me," Jud answered, his voice muffled and hollow from beneath the driftboat.

"My name is Sir Gordon Pendelton and I, I . . ." He tried to finish his introduction, but the dog nearly knocked Sir Gordon over. "I wonder if I might trouble you to call your dog."

"Is it a big black dog or a yellow one?"

"Black."

"Dan!" Jud hollered, and the echo inside the boat made him wince. "Go lie down! Sorry about that, Mister, but he's not my dog. My dog's the yellow one probably asleep by the back porch." Sir Gordon looked over to see Annie the Wonderlab stretched out in the shade, asleep and very much unimpressed by the arrival of either royalty or the Bentley.

Reluctantly, Dan did what he was told. "He's just a pup. I'll be out from under here in just a minute. Doing a little gluing."

"Yes, well, as I was saying, my name is Sir Gor——"

His introduction was again interrupted by a burst of hammering as Jud took a mallet to a makeshift mortise and tenon joint. "Building a boat is one thing, but repairing one, well that's something altogether different. There, that oughta do," he said, finally satisfied with his work. He knelt down and gathered his tools to see that Sir Gordon had his back to him—a big man at eye level, but from ground level he was mountainous.

Jud stepped out from under the dory, a move he'd made a thousand times, but as he did he caught sight of the Bentley, which brought about a double take, which in turn caused him to stand up short of his intent, and he banged his head against the gunnel.

"Sir Gordon Pendelton," he introduced himself once more and extended his hand.

"Well, pleased to meet you Sir Gordon. Jud Clark. I'll shake your hand in a minute, once I get this glue off my fingers."

"I have traveled five thousand miles in the hopes of meeting you, Jud. May I call you Jud?"

"If you want to get my attention," Jud grinned as he grabbed a rag from the workbench. "Five thousand miles—I guess that would be the farthest anyone has traveled to meet me. Sure hope I'm worth it."

Sir Gordon smiled back as if he understood Jud's humor, which he didn't, and continued. Holding out an old leather rod case, he explained, "Inside this case, which has always been in my family's possession, but lost in the Pendelton family archives until just a few months ago, is a fly rod, an old H. L. Leonard fly rod to be more precise, and above its handle is inscribed TRAVER CLARK. In my briefcase I also have fifteen letters from this same Traver C. Clark, to one Lord Pendelton, my great granduncle, who was known in America as D. Downey."

"Well, I'll be! How——"

"Furthermore——"

"Hold it. Hold it. There is someone else who needs to hear this, and he might as well hear it right from the beginning." Jud started for the house. "Excuse me, Sir Gordon. But I have to make a phone call."

"Oh, please, do drop the 'Sir Gordon' nonsense. Knighthood doesn't translate well in America; it barely translates in Britain anymore, for that matter. My friends all call me 'Penny.'"

Halfway across the lawn Jud stopped to realize, "Hey, then that makes you and me some kind of shirttail relatives, doesn't it?"

"Quite right. The genealogy is as follows: Carrie, your great-grandmother, D. Downey's half-sister, married Traver Clark. This makes D. Downey your great-great-uncle. He was my great-great-uncle, but on my mother's side."

"They would put us at the ragged edges of the shirttail. Sounds like we're some of those third cousins, removed a couple of times, the last branches of the family tree, kind of relatives."

"Well, if you want to be more precise, it would make us——"

"No wait. This is getting better and better. I gotta call Henry."

"Henry?" Penny asked.

"Henry Albie."

"There is an Albie mentioned in the letters."

"The Albie in your letters is Henry Albie's great-grandfather."

"He lives here in Travers Corners?"

"About a mile down the road. We were both born and raised right here in the Elkheart."

"This is extraordinary!"

"Come on inside." Jud showed real signs of enthusiasm in some ways: his speech was faster; his arms waved as he spoke, his face was animated; but his gait never broke stride. He was easygoing, more easy than going. Penny followed him, amazed at how anyone could walk so slowly yet speak so quickly. Normally Jud's speech was synchronized to his movements, but at this point he was excited.

Inside, he made the call. "Get over here . . . I don't care . . . This is more important . . . Yeah, Dan's been here all morning." Then he hung up.

"Well, Penny, could I get you anything to drink? Got some cold beers."

"I would love a beer, but I did bring a bottle of scotch, which I left in the shed."

Jud looked at the time. "Well, normally it's a little early for me, but this is no ordinary occasion. I'll go get it. I forgot to turn off the glue gun anyway. Make yourself comfortable." Then Jud was out the porch door. He stepped over Annie, whose participation to this point in all the excitement of foreigners, long-lost relatives, and Bentleys in the drive was but one lazy wag of the tail. Now that she was being stepped over, she managed to lift one eyelid to make sure nothing was being missed. No squirrels in the yard—nothing was being missed.

With Jud gone, Penny became more aware of the room in which he was standing. Dominated by a spiral staircase, the room was large and served as a dining area, kitchen, and living space. He walked over to the stairs to notice the steps were made from halved wagon wheels, oak inlays between the spokes. Wagon tongues formed the handrails. He looked up the spiral, which wound to a second floor and then to the belfry.

The pots and pans over the stove hung from a buggy's wheel. Penny marveled at the cabinetry, the bookshelves, the dining room table and chairs, the trim on the windows, for it was all done from old woods; and Penny judged, from the iron fittings still attached to a lot of the boards that all the furnishings he saw had been made from old wagons and carriages.

"This is fantastic. Bloody incredible, really," Penny said to Jud, who was returning through the back door. "Did you do all this work yourself?"

"Well, most of it. Henry helped me a lot at the beginning. This is the original carriage house from the old homestead. It's the only thing still standing from the Carrie Creek Cattle Company, and it was getting ready to fall over when I bought it," Jud explained as he filled two glasses with ice. "Henry and I tore it to the ground and rebuilt it. Every log is the original except for the bottom timbers." Hearing a truck pulling up the hill, he dropped ice into a third glass.

Henry parked beside the Bentley, then continued to stare at the car as he came up the walk. He was still wearing a leather apron. His hair was ringing wet. His shirt was nearly soaked through. Shoeing the Gillespie's mare was always a wrestling match. She had the worst hooves of any horse in the Elkheart and a mean disposition when it came to horseshoers. He'd managed to shoe her hind feet in about the same amount of time he could have shoed two horses, and her front feet were the tender ones. It was a job he wanted to be over and done with. Jud's call had not been a timely interruption.

Jud, holding the fly rod, followed by Penny, met Henry as he neared the back porch. "This better be good," Henry said. "Ya sounded as if it were some kind of life-or-death situation up here. Then I come up the hill to see a hearse in the driveway."

Jud handed him his scotch. "Henry, meet Sir Gordon Pendelton. Sir Gordon, this is Henry Albie."

"Pleased to meet ya," Henry said.

"'Sir Gordon' is such a dreadful bother. Please, do call me 'Penny,' and it is very good to meet you, Henry."

"Penny has traveled five thousand miles to meet us. He's from England."

"Something sort of told me he wasn't from here," Henry responded in a tone that silently added, "Yeah, and then what happened?"

"He's brought this fly rod with him. You know whose name is on this fly rod?"

"Hard telling." Henry to this point was still waiting for something to make this trip worth it. He thought about the mare. He'd put hobbles on her before he left. She hated to be hobbled and she was going to be even meaner than usual when he got back.

With Penny's permission, Jud took the old Leonard from the case and removed the butt section from its cloth bag, handling the old bamboo as if it were a museum piece, because it was. The red wraps were torn and frayed, and the agate stripping guide was worn through and cracked. The musty smell of old cane went well with scotch whiskey. A vintage rod, one that had been well used before it finally left the river to be filed away with keepsakes and mementos. Jud handed the rod to Henry and he read the name above the wooden grip: TRAVER C. CLARK.

"Henry, Penny here is the great-great-nephew of D. Downey."

"Well, I'll be dipped!" Henry was amazed but you wouldn't have known it by his face; he brought new meaning to the word stoic. When he smiled his mouth barely widened, when he frowned no creases formed, and when he worried nothing showed. Then he realized, "Then this has gotta be the fly rod from the journals."

"Exactly," Jud agreed.

"Journals?" Penny asked.

"The journals Traver kept of their trip through the Yellowstone. In fact he kept a diary right up to the morning of his death. I've got a copy of them upstairs."

"Oh, I would love to see them."

Jud went up to get his volume of the journals, then remembered he had a new copy among the bookshelves and it took a moment to find it. With all the questions he wanted to ask Penny—the how's, and when's, and where's of finding him and Travers Corners, the rod, the Bentley, etc.—

there was one question that came to mind and needed answering before all the rest. If the chance were given, it would be the first question the whole town of Travers would ask. Now, here at the Boat Works, was a man who could lay the one-hundred-year-old mystery to rest. So obvious was the question he was surprised he hadn't asked it already.

But the question came quickly to Henry and he was asking it just as Jud spotted the hardbound book. "Hey, Penny, you wouldn't happen to know what the D. stood for in D. Downey's name, would ya?"

"Damned if I know," was not the answer Henry had hoped to hear.

Jud came out the back door. "You are going to love this book. Traver's drawings are really——" The phone rang. He quickly handed the book to Penny and went back inside to answer, "Hello . . . Yeah . . . Yes . . . Sure . . . You bet . . . Hold on." Jud laid down the receiver and went back out to the porch. "Penny, it's for you."

"I do hope you don't mind, Jud, but I had no other number to leave for my secretary, in case of an emergency, other than yours. I told her that this was to be a fishing vacation and that for nothing *short* of an emergency was I to be bothered." Penny looked at his watch. "It's one o'clock in the morning in London—a good time for an emergency." Showing concern, he went to the phone.

"Just right there on the table, Penny," Jud said after him and then, excitedly, turned to Henry. "I'll bet he knows what the D. stands for."

"He doesn't."

"Did you ask him?"

"Yep. Doesn't have a clue."

They shrugged their shoulders, disappointed and resigned to the fact that the D. in D. Downey would remain a mystery.

Penny couldn't know the significance D. Downey had to the history and everyday life of Travers Corners. Sure, he knew about Mt. D. Downey, the tallest peak in the Elkhearts, but he didn't know that if you want to buy the biggest burger at the Tin Cup Cafe, you order the D. Downey; if you want to take the back way into Reynolds, you go down

D. Downey Road; if you are the best all-around graduating student at the high school, you receive the D. Downey award; and that the town's summer fair is called D. Downey Days, now just a few weeks away.

"That was my wife Gwendolyn," Penny said coming back out to the porch carrying the briefcase. "Calling to see if I had arrived safely. I had been loosely scheduled by my secretary to arrive in Travers Corners yesterday and I would have, but I stopped in Livingston and managed to get on one of your fabled spring creeks. Marvelous fishing, that."

The three of them settled into the shade of the carriage house. There were hundreds of questions to be resolved, but before either Jud or Henry could ask, Penny answered. "How I found out about Travers Corners is an extraordinary story, quite unusual really. But, if I may, I must preface this story with yet another. I must tell you something about D. Downey.

"My great-great-grandfather, Lord Charles Pendelton, lived in the north of England. And like the noblemen of his day, he had a castle, a wife and children, hounds and horses, all the things of wealth. He also had a Scottish mistress, one Elizabeth Downey. The result of this affair was the bastard son, D. Downey. His sister Carrie, incidentally, was fathered in wedlock a few years later. Lord Charles helped secretly with the rearing of his illegitimate boy, never acknowledging him publicly in order to protect the family's name, though everyone in Northumberland knew the truth. D. Downey was raised in Scotland, but in his late twenties he was lured by America and Lord Charles gave him the money to go. His years in America are not very clear to the family; we know that he went to Denver; and we know about his trip to the country north of the Yellowstone, for his stories of that adventure have been kept alive by the family over these many years.

"He was in America five years and then decided to return home. Upon his return he found Lord Charles living alone, his entire family wiped out by influenza. In a strange and very fortuitous move for D. Downey, and for us as his descendants, Charles bestowed full birthrights, his name, and nobility to his only heir. Overnight D. Downey went from the village bastard to Lord Pendelton.

"As a nobleman he married well into the Stewarts. Now, backed by real money, he went about making his fortune doing the things he knew best. He owned taverns, distilleries, breweries, and our family still has money in the whiskey business, transportation mostly."

Henry broke in, "Then, Penny, yer jest the guy I need to see. How about transportin' a little more of that whiskey over this way." They all laughed. Penny poured a second round of scotch and continued.

"So the Pendelton family has prospered. Our holdings and belongings are quite extensive and diversified. The family still owns Pendelton Castle which brings me to the fly rod.

"As you might imagine, a family seven hundred fifty years old, and still rather close knit, mind you, can gather together a great many things, most of which are on display or filed away at the castle. The castle's curator came upon this fly rod and the letters bound together at the bottom of an old trunk, and because they had never been cataloged, he brought them to my father's attention. My father, incidentally, still lives in one wing of the castle. He's old and quite ill and his memory isn't quite as sharp as it used to be, so nothing about the letters meant anything to him. The curator, knowing my love of fishing, contacted me.

"The family knew D. Downey had a sister, a half-sister really, who accompanied him to the States, but beyond that we knew only that she married, lived, and died somewhere in the West; that is, until these letters." Penny took the letters from his briefcase. "Traver's letters are great reading. In one he has a very humorous discourse on the pride and embarrassment of having a town named after him. Very amusing. The last letter is postmarked September 1918. It was Traver notifying D. Downey of Carrie's death.

"So, I went to the map and, by Jove, there was Travers Corners, Montana. The Elkheart Mountains, the Elkheart River, Carrie Creek, Mt. D. Downey, Albie Pass, all the places mentioned in the letters.

"All my life I have wanted to go to Montana and the letters now gave me a reason. You should know that I have an intense fear of flying, so traveling to the States always involves the extra time needed to come by ship.

"A fortnight passed after the discovery of the letters, before I visited my old friend Harold Wellington. I brought the fly rod along for him to take a look at it. Harold is a keen fisherman, and he knows the lore and history surrounding not only the British bamboo rod makers but the Americans as well. Harold has an impressive collection of cane rods and anything else to do with fishing, for that matter. While he was inspecting the rod, which he determined to be an H. L. Leonard, circa 1867, I was telling him about our curator finding the rod, the letters, Travers Corners, D. Downey, and the Carrie Creek Cattle Company, but when I mentioned Carrie Creek, it rang a familiar note for Harold and he went to his library and came back with an article from a magazine, written in 1976, about Jud Clark and the Carrie Creek Boat Works and Guide Service. Harold has an incredible memory for such things, angling and so forth. He's useless, unfortunately, as a barrister, his chosen profession.

"Needless to say, I booked passage for myself and the Bentley the very first chance on the *QE II*. I landed in New York and I drove straight away to Montana. I know I should have forewarned you about my arrival, but I was in desperate need of a holiday. I was coming to Travers Corners. I was going to do a little fishing."

"C'mon over here," Henry said to Penny. "Wanna show you somethin'." Penny, with Jud, followed him off the back porch and across the drive to an opening through the trees; from there they could see all the rooftops of Travers and the river. "Ya can't see Carrie Creek from here, 'cause of the houses and the trees. But, ya see that two-story white house with the green roof next to the water tower?"

"Yes."

"That house sets on the creek, right above where it comes into the Elkheart. Right past there, in that open field, is where Traver, Albie, and D.

Downey camped a hunnert and," Henry paused a moment to do the math, "twenty-two years ago come this September."

Penny looked up from the rooftops to the Elkheart Valley sweeping north and south. Heat waves softened the craggy beginnings of the mountains. The distant cliffs above the river, the cottonwoods following the bends, the ranches along the bench, were lineless distortions in the hot summer haze. The waters of the Elkheart looked clear and peaceful.

"I am in hopes that I will be able to employ you as a guide, Jud. I would very much like to have you take me down the river in one of your lovely boats."

"The fishing has been slow lately," Jud answered. "It's been hot like this every day for a week. But, sure we can take you float fishing, just so you know that the river has been pretty dead; usually is this time of year. The upper-meadow stretches of Carrie Creek might be pretty good, though; we could have some luck up there." Henry agreed.

"Slow is precisely the speed I will be hoping to achieve this vacation, Jud. My life as of late has been one of great stress—one daughter, unfortunately, going through a messy divorce; one daughter about to have her first child; a son who at twenty-four is somewhere in Nepal 'finding himself.' Gwendolyn, God bless her, is trying to hold everything and everyone together and is buckling under the strain.

"The trucking business has been crippled by strikes, and for the last three months I have been embroiled in union meetings.

"In short, if the fishin' is slow, gentlemen, I will be most thankful to be slow right along with it. Slow: the very sound of the word is quite enchanting."

(*Author's note:* Now that I have all the generalities in place, the history outlined, Penny's character sketched in, there is really nothing more to report over the next five hours other than the details. If I were a novelist instead of short-story writer, I would now chronicle every spoken word, every gesture, nuance, and thought by our three characters; but I would really like to get on with the story.

I would, naturally, report on anything from this evening that pertains to the story at hand, but much of the time was spent reading from Traver's letters and journals. The letters, as it turned out, were just the abbreviated news from the journals. The journals, which were encapsulated back in the introduction, are available for $9.95 and are sold at most bookstores and all the state parks and museums. So, dear reader, I chose not to report anything more from this night, as I feared I would end up repeating myself, you know, like a novelist.

I think all you need know is that the night was not lengthy and by nine o'clock they had switched to coffee. This was done without choice as the scotch was long gone; also know that the bottle was emptied in a relatively short period of time and that a certain level of frivolity was reached.

Oh, there was one reading from Traver's journals I should share with you, not that you will learn much more than you already know, but it adds a certain flavor, if not a little foreshadowing, to the old fly rod and how it came to be D. Downey's. It was written September 19th, 1873:

D. Downey and I fished the tributary to the main river today; the stream we have named "Carrie Creek." He is such a wonder with a fly rod. His fly lands so neatly and quietly on the water, while mine lands in a cat's cradle. He fools the fish while the fish make a fool out of me. He caught fifteen fish today and they will be supper tonight. I caught three, one accidentally, but when it all goes right, when I do manage to make a proper cast, it is such a marvelous sport. I have decided that at the end of this adventure, when we are back in Denver, I will give this fly rod, a Leonard, given to me by my father, to D. Downey. He admires it so.

Well, that brings me to the end of the author's note, a five-paragraph parenthetical that saved pages of repetitive dialogue, not to mention a few trees. Let's see, where should I pick up the tale? I know. There was a rather good moment just as Penny and Henry were getting ready to leave, Penny to his room at the Take 'er Easy Motel, and Henry back to a hobbled mare that he would now finish shoeing in the morning.)

From their hillside view outside the Boat Works the three of them paused to look past the glow of town to the ranches along the bench whose yard lights were beginning to show now, much as the first stars appear, flickering, the night not yet dark enough to carry their light. Streaks of peach-colored light lay along the last horizon and the mountains and valley were just varying shades of the last of the day. The shapes of things easily known by their lines were now lost in the shadows, muted like a Chatham.

"Can you imagine Travers Corners one hundred years ago? Not much more than a stage stop, and nothing else for as far as you could see," Jud mused.

The three of them stood looking out over the valley; coursing back through more than a century of bloodlines, to the headwaters of the gene pool, to a time pictured differently by each one.

For Henry the past was an easy image. Cowboyin' in the Old West. Make it into town for Saturday nights. The wildlife. The wilderness. The solitude. No bullshit bureaucracy. No tax man. "I'd go back in a heartbeat," he said, not a hint of hesitation in his voice.

Penny, whose only reference to the Old West was the occasional western over the BBC, could only picture the town as John Ford might have framed it: tumbleweeds rolling through a wooden town, with two horses tied to the saloon. But somewhere, and he felt it deep in his chest, were the prideful inner stirrings of his newly found history—that his forefather, D. Downey, had been here when the West was wild, and he had been one of the first into an untamed country. The pioneering spirit mixed strangely with the genetics of his other heritage—seven hundred years of nobility. Somewhere deep in the DNA he was Wichita-on-Thames; he was High Noon on Big Ben; Wyatt Earp at the U.K. Corral; John Wayne riding to hounds; and Cromwell against the Comanches. "I think it would be marvelous, if time travel did exist, to go back for a visit. But I don't know if I could take the isolation of it all."

Jud thought of the bygone wilderness. The great Alone—timeless days, lonely nights. All work, little leisure. No rock and roll; no Mel Brooks; no Häagen-Dazs; no Diane Keaton. He thought of the open range, where seldom was heard a discouraging word, or any word, for that matter, and the skies were not cloudy all day, the weather being the only change in one's life. And sure, the buffalo roamed, but not so much for fresh grass—they were just looking for something to do.

"Well, I'll settle for the here and now," Jud said, smiling. "A hundred years ago the only fish in the valley were whitefish and cutthroat. I don't know if that would be worth going back for. What would you say to a little fishing tomorrow, Penny? Rainbows and browns."

"I would say that should be highest among the priorities."

It was decided. They would meet at the Tin Cup in the morning for breakfast, then it would be an afternoon of fishing up above Johnson Springs, where Carrie Creek winds through the meadows.

They said their good-nights and Penny followed Henry down the hill to the motel.

Working the night shift at the Take 'er Easy was Wendy Smith, one of the great phone gossips in Travers; and after Penny was checked in, Henry slipped Wendy the news. "Sir Gordon here is the great-great-nephew of D. Downey."

Wendy waited for her chance and while Penny, with Henry, went about unloading the car, she got Henry alone. She didn't waste a second. She went right to the question: "Does he know what the D. stands for?"

"He doesn't have a clue."

After Penny was settled in and Henry had left for home, Wendy went to the phones; the gossip network was fully activated. The wires were lit and burning with the news that the great-great-nephew of D. Downey was in town. This was big news in a town not known for news.

Wendy had done her job well and reported the story with great accuracy. After all, she had Penny's motel registration form to go by as she spread the word: Name—Sir Gordon Pendelton; Address—Henley-on-Thames, England; Make of Car—Bentley.

But by morning, as the regulars crowded into the Tin Cup, the rumor had taken on many different mutations, the most popular one being: Name—Lord Pennington; Address—this ranged from Ireland to Wales; Make of Car—no doubt about it, the guy was driving a Rolls. However, two parts of the news managed to remain intact despite the whorl of rumor, and those were: D Downey's great-great-nephew was in Travers and he didn't know what the D. stands for.

On his way to breakfast Penny dropped the Bentley off at Ed's garage. Ed was there as was son Pete. Penny outlined in great detail what needed to be done to the car, but Ed was quick to explain, "I've never worked on a car like this one. Hell, I've never even seen a car like this one. I don't know if——"

"Nonsense," Penny interrupted. "Jud and Henry have both verified your mechanical skills as first rate. If you do have any trouble, you may consult this maintenance manual," and he handed Ed a leather-bound, three-inch-thick book. "There are some specialized tools when dealing with an old Bentley, and you will find those tools in the boot; as well as every other tool you may need. She should be fine beneath the bonnet, save the oil being changed, but maybe just give it all a bit of a look, won't you? On the inside of the manual is written the phone number of my mechanic in London. If you have any questions, just give him a call, reversing charges, of course, and he will talk you through any difficulties you may encounter. I don't expect to have any problems, really, as I had her tuned top-to-toe before I left. But, I will be here for nearly a month and I plan to put many miles on the old girl, fishing miles, mind you, so I am quite certain she will need some form of attention. She's quite an old girl, you know."

"Okay," Ed agreed, "but I——"

"Splendid." Then Penny turned to the Pistol, who was spinning a basketball on his finger. "Warm water, mild soap for her wash; something like a dish soap. Soft cloths. You will find a special wax that I use on her in the boot as well. Very good then, and thanks so much." And Penny headed across Main Street to the Tin Cup Cafe, where Henry, with Jud, had just taken a table.

Pete would have gone right to work on the car, but instead he took his ball and did a slow dribble around the Bentley, admiring her classic lines surely, but mostly he was looking for something that would tell him where and what the boot might be. Ed was busy looking for a bonnet.

The Tin Cup was buzzing with the news. Henry and Jud had been cornered by Junior McCracken, who, as Mayor, had a keen interest in the arrival of Sir Gordon Pendelton. If you can't picture how one man could corner two, you have never seen Junior McCracken pace. He paces normally, but when he's excited, and he was excited, Junior moves like a false cast. "He was in my store yesterday. Of course, I didn't know who he was. Said he was going to do a little fishing. Bought a bottle of scotch. Great big guy. Has no idea what the D. stands for, you say?"

Jud and Henry watched Junior pace back and forth in front of their table. "Hasn't the foggiest," Jud answered.

"How long do you think he will stay?"

"Said he was going to be here quite a while, a month anyways," Henry said.

"Then he will be here for D. Downey Days." Now Junior was really thrilled. As chairman of the Fair Committee he could see Sir Gordon now at the head of the parade. "Is he the sort of man who might be interested in being our Grand Marshal?"

"Why don't you ask him yerself?" Henry nodded to the front of the cafe as Penny came through the door.

Waves of whispers, silences, and mutterings spread through the cafe as Penny walked briskly, unaware that he was at the center of everyone's attention, to the back table where Henry and Jud were seated. "Good morning, gentlemen," Penny greeted, nodding to Junior.

"Sir Gordon Pendelton, I'd like you to meet Junior McCracken. Junior, here, is our Mayor, our pharmacist, chief retailer, and leading citizen; and one of the keenest fisherman of Travers Corners." Jud chose "keenest" as his adjective for its ambiguity: it depicted Junior as an avid angler while masking the fact that Junior, while persistent, was one of the worst, if not the unluckiest, fishermen in the valley.

"We sort of met already, haven't we? You are the chap who sold me the whiskey."

"That's right."

"A pleasure to meet you, Junior, I am sure."

"Well, how are you this morning, Penny?"

"I am in great spirits, Jud, thank you, and at your service," Penny said sitting down next to Henry.

"Sit down and join us, Junior," Jud invited.

"Ah, Jeez, I can't. Some sort of flu bug has hit town, the grammar school mostly. Tomorrow it will be the high school. Next day the town. Quite a few of the parents started getting it yesterday. I'll be filling prescriptions for Parapectolin all day long."

"Sir Gordon," asked Junior as he resumed his pacing, "I was hoping, and I am sure I speak for the whole town of Travers Corners, that, ah, providing you were still going to be here, and all, on September 17th—that would be two weeks come Saturday—ah, well, that you might consider being the Grand Marshal for the D. Downey Days parade."

"I would love to, that would be absolutely marvelous."

Junior was pleased, anxious, and frustrated—frustrated because he knew that as soon as he left, the conversation would turn to fishing, and Junior loved to talk about fishing. He had stopped his pacing and was now bouncing up and down on his toes. "Listen, I gotta go. Thanks, Sir Gordon." He started to leave but came back to the table and said, "Sure is a shame about the D. in D. Downey's name."

"Bloody shame."

Looking over to the grill to see Bonnie substitute-cooking for Sarah, Jud looked up to Sally, who was their waitress, and asked, "Where's Sarah today?"

"Down with the flu and madder 'n a hornet about it. Are you really the great-great-nephew of D. Downey?" Sally couldn't help herself.

"I am."

"Well, that's amazin', real amazin',"—then Sally took their order. The entire cafe was trying not to stare at Sir Gordon and, although he couldn't hear any of their dialogue over the banging of plates and general restaurant noise, Penny knew he was the subject of every conversation. "My being here seems to have stirred a certain amount of interest, hasn't it?"

"Well, you have to realize about D. Downey in this town," Jud answered. Then he and Henry filled Penny in on the significance of his forefather in Travers Corners: about how the town sits in the shadow of Mt. D. Downey, tallest peak in the Elkhearts; about how on Sunday the town's Baptists gather at the D. Downey First Baptist Church and get there by turning off Main up D. Downey Street.

"There's D. Downey Days, the D. Downey Rodeo, et cetera. And," Henry said, pointing to the Tin Cup's menu, "the D. Downey Burger," which had a caricature of D. Downey high atop a mountain of French fries. The conversation then turned to fishing and the plans were made for the rest of the day over steak and eggs. A few of the townspeople came over and welcomed Penny to town, all of them asking him if he had a chance to see Traver's journals.

"No," he would answer, "but later this afternoon I do plan to stop and see them. I read some of the journals last night, but I am very anxious to see the originals. But, today, Henry and Jud have been kind enough to ask me fishing."

And by midmorning that's just where they were—fishing, fanned out on the long winding bends of Carrie Creek, in the high country, in the rainbow water above the beaver ponds. The mist that blanketed the valley had lifted; the day was warming.

They were wading the willowed walls, the hallowed halls of a dry fly meadow stream, where lightly colored mayflies were drifting past the fallen branches now yellowing with the advent of fall; around the exposed rocks still drying from last night's frost; through the reflections of mountains, puff clouds, and sky; around the bends filled with long, flowing moss; above the shadowy undercut banks; and among the first fallen leaves of autumn. Mayflies were everywhere but the trout were being very slow to notice. Nary a rise.

It may well have been hot down in the Elkheart Valley during the day, but it was definitely cooling at night. September was only two days away. But here at the headwaters of Carrie Creek, about seventeen hundred feet above Travers Corners, autumn was imminent—it had frosted four nights running. In the aspen groves above the meadows, glints of gold, leaves edged by the cold, lay still but for an occasional flutter.

Moving along slowly, wading a long, sweeping turn, came Penny, a mountain of a man, and his reflection was the befitting mirror image of the Elkheart Range, now broken by ripples, the wakes to his movements. Mt. D. Downey stood straight ahead of him, rising up from the mouth of the meadow. He was not even slightly disappointed that the fish were not active, and was enjoying himself immensely. The beauty of the place was remarkable. He felt unencumbered by business or family and all their attached problems. What a nightmare year it had been.

Penny made the occasional cast, prospecting the banks and behind boulders, but nothing. He could see Henry, a few bends upstream from him, crouched down on one knee, secreting himself in the tall grass, and casting deliberately. Henry had a particular fish in mind. Looking downstream, Penny saw no sign of Jud. A rise registered in the corner of his eye.

Thinking seriously about a short nap, warming in the sun, lying on a log, Jud was watching the creek; a most familiar bend; an old haunt. Right now he was caught up in the beauty of this place, and even though it was a setting he came to every fall, the valley remained breathtaking year in and year out. Sometimes you don't know whether to fish or just stare. He would fish in a while.

He was thinking about how incredible the last twenty-four hours had been, with the arrival of Sir Gordon Pendelton and all; thinking how things had somehow traveled full circle. One hundred and twenty-seven years after their forebears had fished here, the three of them were fishing Carrie Creek. It was almost impossible.

The trout began feeding slowly, then more fish came out of the shadows to dine, and soon one fish after another were coming to the surface. Mayflies were being taken with reckless abandon, and there were some very sizable backs breaching for dries. Any thoughts of a nap had vanished. Perhaps he would fish now and stare later.

Yes, the mayflies were dancing; they had taken the floor, and none of their fancy steps were lost on the trout. It was like a conga line at the Rainbow Room; the flies were all in a row and the trout were filling their dance cards. Every fish in the creek was up and eating and Henry was casting to his third trout, landing his first, missing his second. His first cast and the fish took. A good-sized rainbow ran with his line downstream.

It had been a long time since Penny had seen anything to rival this fishing. There had been one afternoon on the Teste, but that was years ago. He was no stranger to the pastime of fly fishing and had neatly landed two trout. He marveled at the gluttony of these fish and prayed they would remain as careless for the rest of the day. He was long overdue for such a day.

Standing on a bend with twenty fish rising, Penny laughed out loud; he couldn't help himself. He missed a take. He cast to another fish and had him on, a heavy fish who came three feet out of the water on his first jump. "Marvelous. Bloody marvelous."

And so his day went. It grew warmer. The hatch tapered off, then stopped around one-thirty. But then came the spinners, spent, lying facedown in the film; and though the trout weren't coming as easily as they had earlier, they were still coming, and with enough regularity to make every part of the bend, pool, riffle, and glide a temptation to his cast. For he knew that if he fished it properly, the fish would be there and they'd be willing.

The afternoon was windless and warm, and the freeze from the night before had wiped out the mosquitoes. There were a few deerflies around to give you a nip, but other than that the day was perfection. Around five o'clock, Penny had fished up until he was opposite the car. Henry could be seen a few hundred yards off coming back through the field. Jud hadn't been seen by either fisherman all day.

Easing into the creek, stripping line slowly from his reel, Jud was wading in well behind several trout feeding upstream. He was belly-deep; a few leaves floated down and pinned themselves briefly against his waders, then washed free. In the midst of several smaller fish a large rainbow was dining in the bubble line.

It wasn't a question that a fish was going to take, it was just a matter of luck as to which one, a big one or a small one. Luck was the key word here; luck is the key, period. Good luck, bad luck, a run of luck, a piece of luck. Life is luck and the luckless. When one goes fishing, he certainly hopes to have good luck. When one goes gambling, he wants Lady Luck to blow on his dice. On a honky-tonk Saturday night, men and women take to the dance floor, women in the hopes of lucking into a man, while the men are just there to get lucky. Jud figured, as he began to cast out his line, that perhaps luck comes to you in thirds: a third of the time you're lucky; a third of the time you're unlucky; and the remaining third falls into the prosaic, indistinguishable days brought in by Philistines; the meat-and-potato days served by pedestrians; days when the status is quo; days when the bookies, who hang out at the corner of Humdrum and Mundane, give even odds—that your day will be normal, ordinary, average. The kind of day when luck of any kind ignores you.

Jud made his cast and luck was with him. Luck, in that he was lucky to be doing what he loved best, and that he had a fish on his very first cast, but it wasn't the full-blown luck he had hoped for. It was one of the smaller fish, maybe the smallest in the group, and its thrashing sent the big one, three pounds at least, scurrying downstream between his legs. Watching it go instead of keeping an eye on his line, his fish had managed to wrap itself in the deep water, costing him his last spinner imitation.

"How ya doin', Penny?" Henry greeted.

Standing in the middle of a long, sweeping bend, Penny answered, "It has been splendid. Brilliant, really. And you?"

"It was pretty darn good, I don't mind telling ya."

"It's been slower in the last hour, didn't you find?"

"Here, Penny," Henry said climbing down the bank. "Let's you and me exchange rods. Mine's all rigged up with a hopper." The rods traded, Henry waved him upstream. "Fish 'er tight to the bank all the way to the next bend. Pay special attention when ya get up by those two rocks. There's some truly dangerous trout up there." It was Henry's favorite stretch. He looked to see Jud coming out of the willows way downstream. He then walked over to his truck, opened the cooler, and grabbed a beer from the ice.

By the time Jud got to the car, Penny had worked halfway up the bend without a strike. "Well, letting Penny fish your bend, are you?"

"You bet." It was a short answer but it came with a nod of his head, and Jud, who knew Henry better than anyone, recognized the look in his eye, which meant that despite the Bentley, the Royalty, and the rest, Henry thought Penny was all right. If he hadn't thought so, there was no way he would have given up his favored stretch of water. They leaned against the truck and watched Penny fish upstream.

When Penny finally hooked one, he was a hundred feet away, just behind the two rocks. The fish came out of the water, and even from that distance, Henry and Jud knew it was large. "Looks like Penny's hooked inta one of the more dangerous ones," Henry said.

Sweeping in a long arc, the fish and line creased the water. The trout broke water once more, this time its motion looking like not so much of a jump really, but an unintentional departure brought about by the sheer speed of her run. She was heading downstream. She ran until she was even with where Henry and Jud were standing, then swung headlong back into the current. Through the swirls and boils the rainbow's bright sides flared, then disappeared, blending back into the waters.

Penny was following, reeling carefully as he waded downstream and angling his body toward the shallower water. Henry grabbed his net from the back of the truck. Jud walked down to the river for a better view.

The fish moved and jumped once more. This time Jud got a good look at him. "She's a big one, Penny."

Penny, who was slightly out of breath, yelled, "Oh this is marvelous! Bloody marvelous!"

The trout took another run, jumping three times, trying to shake free but to no avail—she was hooked too well. Henry positioned himself below the rainbow with his net at the ready. The current played on the hemp basket as Penny's rod tip guided the rainbow into the net.

"That's as good a fish as I've seen come out of Carrie Creek all summer. Nineteen inches," Henry guessed.

Taking the net from Henry, Penny reached in with his pliers and plucked his hook free. Cradling the trout, while admiring her colors of chrome, crimson, and dark green, he removed her from the netting. With his rod tucked beneath his arm, he moved the fish naturally back and forth in the current until she fully revived. He then loosened his hold and the trout slowly swam back into the depths.

"That moment was worth the trip," Penny said, splashing water on his sunburned face. "I have a feeling Henry knew something about this bend. Giving a stranger the best water goes well beyond the expected limits of etiquette. Thank you so much for the privilege of letting me fish here."

"You bet," Henry said. "My pleasure." Then he turned to Jud. "How'd you do today? You sure as hell couldn't of fished much water—you came out of the willers the same place ya went in."

"Well, it was great. I would fish for a while, then I would stare for a while. This has been such an incredible day. Fished the same bend all day. I'd land a fish, spook the water, wait five minutes, and they were all back up an' eating. Incredible fishing. Missed a good one. I did, however, put those five-minute delays to good use, I want you to know: I napped, imagined, wondered, and came up with a theory or two."

Henry changed the subject. He knew it was too late in the afternoon to get started on one of Jud's theories. "We better be heading back. Why don't we meet at the Tin Cup for supper?" It was agreed—supper at seven.

Back in Travers, Henry went on home, Jud went to the Boat Works, and Penny, as planned, went down to the library to see the journals. Unfortunately, an hour before, Janet Hillyer had been in the library with her five kids. The flu bug was rampant. Five pairs of virus-coated hands had just visited the drinking fountain. Penny, slightly parched from a day in the sun, stopped at the fountain. Contagion. He didn't have a chance.

The original journals—setting down the daily accounts of Traver and D. Downey and their trip into the Elkheart with their hired guide, Albie—were as fascinating as Jud and Henry had promised. The sketches were wonderful. Traver was a fairly accomplished artist. But, as Penny had been told, the entries from their trip into the Yellowstone, then on to the Elkheart Valley, were the ones that held the most interest. For after Traver and Carrie had settled in the valley, the journals quit being a diary and became more of a ledger, recording cattle prices, expenses, and income. Penny read for nearly an hour. He was allowed to thumb through the originals, as Sandy Gamblin, the town's librarian, removed the journals from their glass case—a very special privilege, but after all, Penny was the great-great-nephew of D. Downey. He was able to see all the drawings, to see how the valley looked—without a building, without a road, without the plowed fields. A pencil drawing of Carrie Creek, Mt. D. Downey, sketched more than a century before, covered one full page. Penny found it quite remarkable that he had fished the same meadow stream only that afternoon.

By seven o'clock, the time he had planned to meet up with Henry and Jud at the Tin Cup Cafe, Penny was not particularly hungry; in fact, his stomach was feeling slightly queasy. During dinner he went from queasy to feverish. He reluctantly excused himself from the evening, as the talk promised to move to fly fishing. "I really believe that this might be the beginning of the illness afflicting your town. I think it would be best if I headed back to the motel."

Henry drove Penny down to the Take 'er Easy, while Jud called Doc Higgins for whatever it was he was prescribing.

"This virus is a vicious little thing," Doc said. "I'll call Junior and have him put together a few pills. Say, what kind of fella is this Sir Gordon Pendelton? His arrival sure has caused quite a stir!"

"He's a good guy; a bit stuffy, very proper, stiff upper lip, very regimental, and all that sort of thing, old bean," Jud answered, mimicking a British accent. "He's a good fisherman. You'll meet him, Doc. I'm going to have you up this weekend. Have all the local fishing types there—Henry, you, Junior, Lee Wright. Saturday night all right?"

"Sounds good to me."

As it turned out, Junior delivered the prescription himself. The pills helped somewhat, but there was nothing Penny really could do but ride out the infection. The virus ran its course. There was no sleep. He spent his time mostly in the bathroom, keeping both ends close to the bowl.

The next morning Henry stopped by the Taker 'er Easy to see if there was anything Penny needed. Jud called him on the phone.

It was around eleven-thirty when Penny stepped from the shower. He was feeling better but still pretty lousy. He'd just finished dressing when Sarah Easterly stopped by with some soup. "Jud asked me to bring you over something easy to eat. I had this bug yesterday; what a nightmare. But, if you get some rest, and you drink liquids, you'll be feeling okay by tomorrow. Listen to me—I sound like a doctor."

"I do feel better, Sarah, and thank you so much for the soup. It was very kind of you."

"Gotta run. I got the lunch crowd coming. I'll see you on Saturday night. Jud's having a little get-together, and I'm helping him with the dinner. Sure am looking forward to visiting with you, Penny."

Later in the afternoon, Penny felt much better. Leaving the motel in the late afternoon, he went for a walk along the river. *How marvelous*, he thought, *every one so far had been kindhearted; staying around the town of Travers Corners will be a great pleasure.* As he strolled along a well-worn path, he formulated his plans. The very first thing he was going to do when he got back to his room was call the Boat Works and see if either Jud or Henry could take him float-fishing tomorrow down this lovely river before him. Stopping for a moment to watch the water and its currents, he felt a little lightheaded; perhaps some of this sensation was the residue of his contagion, but mostly his giddiness derived from the realization that there were four weeks of uninterrupted fishing ahead of him, and what a grand time it would be.

On his return to the motel he called Jud, and the plans were made. Henry would take him fishing tomorrow. The next day he would go fishing on his own, back to the meadows and Carrie Creek. Then on Saturday, Jud would float him on a different stretch of the river, down in the canyon. Fish were smaller there, but, according to Jud, Log Jam Canyon was too beautiful a place to miss.

The following morning Penny awakened feeling surprisingly close to normal and excited about the day. The phone rang in his room—the overseas operator had a call for Sir Gordon Pendelton. Wendy was at the desk and patched it through to his room and, of course, listened in.

When the Bentley pulled into the drive, it did so nearly an hour later than scheduled. Henry was helping Jud move around a few driftboats, to make room for the one just finished. Henry thought of the day as the oddest combination of things. First, the coincidence of the day's timing was overwhelming: the fact that over a century ago Albie had guided Traver, and now he was about to guide Sir Gordon. He also looked at the day as fortuitous since Penny had insisted on paying for it. Henry would have gladly done it for nothing, but if a guy who drives a Bentley wanted to pay him the full price for a day's guiding, well, that was all right, too.

The Bentley rolled to a stop. Penny walked over to where they were working. He was dressed not as a man about to go fishing but as he was when he first arrived. His walk was a sullen walk; he was stooped at the shoulder, looking so deflated that he appeared as a much smaller man. Drawn and sorrowful, he said, "I must return to England. I am leaving this afternoon."

"You're kidding!"

"Ya jest got here."

"Why?"

"This morning I received a call. The news was bad. My younger brother, Peter, represents the family in the largest part of our business, the trucking business. Last night he suffered a heart attack. He will be fine, the doctors have assured us, but he will not be returning to work for quite some time. There is no one in the family to step in, but me, I'm afraid.

"As of midnight Sunday night, if no agreements have been made, the lorry drivers will strike. In short, gentlemen, it is very tense right at the moment, and it is critical that I return."

"Must be critical," Henry said, "if they're gonna git *you* on an airplane. And yer timin'—couldn't hardly 'a been any worse. It was cold last night, down to twenty-eight at my house. The river's sure to come to life. The big browns will be out and about. Now I ain't kiddin' ya."

"Unfortunately, I will be representing not only the family's holdings, but those of the investors, shareholders, and bankers. Millions of pounds are at stake. So, these aforementioned people would show little understanding, let me assure you of this, if their best interests were not being represented because their spokesperson was absent out of a fear of heights, or that he was on holiday and the fishing was just too good to leave.

"I have favors to ask of you both. Instead of guiding me this afternoon, Henry, would you mind terribly taking me to the airport in Missoula? I insist on paying you, of course, the same fee as if you had guided me."

"Well, sure, only you don't have to . . ."

"I insist."

"What are you going to do with the Bentley?" Jud asked.

"This brings me to the second favor. Would it be possible that one of you could store her for me until I make further arrangements?"

"Sure," Jud said, "I can move a boat or two around and put her in the shed."

"That is most kind of you. There is a tarpaulin in the boot. If you could just see that she is securely covered?"

"You bet."

"I will be more than happy to pay a storage fee."

"Forget it."

"I was really looking forward to my time in your valley. Your hospitality has been wonderful. But know this, gentlemen, I will be coming back—not this year, and next year will be impossible, but perhaps the year after. In the meantime, Jud, would you be kind enough to build one of your lovely river dories and ship it to me at this address?" Penny asked as he handed Jud a business card.

"Getting it there will cost more than the boat."

"That will be fine. Make it your very best model. I will be the envy of every salmon fisherman on the Tweed in such a boat." Penny looked at his watch. "Well, I suppose we had better be off. My flight is at one. Henry, if you would be kind enough to drive, it might prove easier for me to familiarize you with the old girl's idiosyncrasies."

Jud had reasons to tag along: There were some errands he could run in Missoula; he also needed more varnish and several other supplies only a city could provide. But most of all, he went along because no matter what, he was not going to miss Henry at the wheel of a Bentley.

The drive to Missoula was uneventful; for most of the trip Penny fell silent, and other than to tell Henry about another feature to the car, said very little. Instead, he just stared out the window, pensive about the negotiations ahead, saddened by having to leave the valley, and angry to have his fly-fishing holiday end before it had a chance to begin.

Henry turned the Bentley onto I-90. "Should make 'er into Missoula in about twenty minutes."

Sensing Penny's mood from the backseat, Jud leaned forward and tried to lighten the conversation, taking it back to the night Penny first arrived, to a night full of unbelievable events, to the meadows at Carrie Creek. "I still can't quite believe how this whole thing came about. The old Leonard. You coming all this way. Finding Henry and me. The coincidences are remarkable. The chances of something like this happening seem almost impossible."

"Yep, this is the kind of thing that could only happen in Ripley's. A thousand-to-one shot for sure." Henry continued, "Well, at least we had one day of fishin', and a good day of fishin' at that. That was one truly great fish you took there at the end, Penny—best one I've seen in quite a few years.

"There is one thing I do regret," Henry said, turning his head to look at Jud. Then his eyes shot back to the road ahead. Driving the Bentley was making him a little edgy; it drove beautifully but it was going to take a while to get used to driving from the right side, really the wrong side, of the car. "I mean, you comin' to Travers and us all gettin' together, goin' fishin', that's all been great and everything, but I sure do wish you would'a known what the D. stood for in D. Downey—that's somethin' that's puzzled the town forever."

"Henry, I *do* know what the D. stands for and I told you the night of my arrival."

"But, I asked, and you said ya didn't know."

"'*Damned* if I know' I believe was my precise answer."

"Okay, then, but——" Henry was cut short as Penny nodded his head slightly toward him while raising his eyebrows and widening his eyes: the facial gesture that everyone reads as "Do you get it now?"

"The D. in D. Downey's name stands for 'Damned if I know'?" Jud queried, half shouting, his voice filled with disbelief.

"Damned If I Know Downey," Henry repeated, then started laughing;

but he stopped when he saw in Penny's face that his laughter was not being appreciated.

"That is the regrettable truth, old chaps, and it's something the family has tried very hard to forget. It is a subject we certainly don't talk about, let alone elaborate on." But Penny had acquiesced with a shrug of his shoulders to their collective curiosities.

"That's how the story goes, and it's been handed down now for a hundred years, so please realize it's no longer a story, really, as much as it is folklore." Penny turned slightly in his seat so he could talk easily to Jud as well and continued, "Perhaps, you might remember from the other night when I was explaining how D. Downey came to be the illegitimate son of Lord Pendelton?"

They both nodded.

"Well then, according to the story, when D. Downey's mother asked His Lordship what surname she should give the boy, Pendelton or Downey, he became enraged and told her that no bastard would have the name Pendelton. He was to be a Downey. She then followed him out to his carriage, asking him what he would favor as a first name. 'Damned if I know' was his answer; damned if he cared was his tone. And waiting in the carriage was his new mistress.

"Hence, in a rage of tears, Elizabeth vowed to do just that. When D. Downey came into this world, she named him 'Damned If I Know Downey.' She saw the boy and his name as vengeful reminders to His Lordship of his transgressions, and everyone her son knew and met would know the story of her abandonment. She gave no thought as to how unbearable the name would be for her son to live with, what it would be like to be greeted everyday and in that same breath be labeled a bastard. The name stuck with D. Downey until he grew larger and stronger than anyone in the village; then no one called him 'Damned If I Know' or they would be knocked for six.

"In America no one knew what the D. stood for and he told no one. When he returned to Scotland and took over the castle and the Pendelton name, the D. was dropped entirely. And now the story has drifted back into a small piece of history, a footnote in an *almost* forgotten volume, and that is how the family would like to keep it."

Jud looked amazed; almost stunned. Henry was hysterical, but his face didn't show a thing.

With everything explained, Penny was eager to change the subject. D. Downey's origins always made him a little uncomfortable and that—coupled with the fact that the airport, his waiting plane, and flying were only minutes away—was making him downright edgy. Soon he would be at home, embroiled in union battles, and refereeing family squabbles. Instead of fishing, instead of the solace of Carrie Creek, instead of his four-week holiday, he now had a month of hell awaiting him. He asked, "Jud, would you mind opening up the bar, that wooden cabinet, right there in front of you? That's right. Could you please pour me a rather large whiskey, and one for yourself, if you like."

For the rest of the drive, conversation lapsed into the pre-airport small talk about landings, arrivals, and times. They were also more conscious of the time, and Henry sped the Bentley up to eighty.

They pulled into the airport with seventeen minutes left till departure. Back from the ticket counter, all his luggage checked, five minutes to take-off, Penny stuffed his ticket and passport back into his sport coat. "I'll be back, gentlemen. Thank you for your kindness and hospitality. Looking forward tremendously to my river dory, Jud, and a pleasure fishing with you, Henry. We shall do it again, I promise. And, if either of you ever wishes to visit England, I would very much like to have you as my guest at Pendelton Castle. You would enjoy it there, the grounds are lovely. I'll take you to a chalkstream that's quite marvelous."

As Penny turned and walked toward Gate B, Jud shouted after him, "I'll get your boat there somehow, even if I have to row it." Henry waved and Penny blended into the airport montage, everything and everybody in motion.

After picking up a few odds and ends in Missoula, Henry was glad to pull back onto I-90. He had grown uncomfortable in town; driving the Bentley brought about too many stares. "Don't think I'd wanna car like this one. I mean I can appreciate what a fine car it is, now don't git me wrong. It's just, well, did ya see how every time we came to a stop, people were strainin' for a look, hopin' that a somebody would be steppin' out, 'cause only a somebody would drive a car like this?"

"All you need to be a somebody these days is a look," Jud prodded, "something unusual, something never seen before; and Henry, I'm almost positive that the combination of horseshoer, in guide's attire, at the wheel of a Bentley, is a look no one's seen before."

Having no time to change, Henry drove in his guiding clothes, which were the same as his farrier's clothes, but without the leather apron. He hadn't shaved, but he never shaves on guide days—it's bad luck. He was suspenders and tattered shirt instead of braces and tattersall check. He was boots and not brogans. And where a neat English cap should sit, sat his gnarled and crusty Stetson.

"No, Henry, I would say, without any hesitation, that you are not the average man behind the wheel of a Bentley."

"And glad I ain't. I mean when I think about Penny's life and what he is goin' back to—shit. Havin' to live and work in that insanity—I don't think so. Penny might git to drive a Bentley but the cost ain't worth it. I'll just stick to shoein' and guidin', and though she's no luxury liner, my pickup still takes me where I need to go."

"Penny was all right, though. Sure, he was a rich guy, but he wasn't a *painful* rich guy. In fact, I liked him; but then again," Jud laughed, "we are kin."

"Yeah, he was all right. Surprised me, even. One thing I can't understand, though—don't you think he was a might sensitive about D. Downey bein' a bastard? It ain't that big a deal and it was over a hunnert years ago. I mean you take away all the bastards born out of Montana's history and this place would be nothin' but gophers and buffalo."

Jud laughed. "What are we going to tell the folks back in Travers about the D.; about the 'Damned If I Know'?"

"We tell 'em just what we found out."

"Well, that's all fine and good," Jud answered, trying to suppress a smile and losing, "but we take the mystery out of D. Downey's name and there's going to be some serious repercussions. I mean, eliminate the initial and you'll have all the Baptists in Travers turning up Damned If I Know Street instead of D. Street to get to their church—now named after the valley's most famous bastard. Travers Corners will no longer sit in the shadow of Mt. D. Downey; it'll sit in the shadow of a son of a bitch. The town fair, the high school mascot, Montana's history books, map makers, et cetera. Many things will have to change."

Henry started to laugh, thinking about the town's leading Baptist, "Etta May Harper ever got wind of this she would coronary on out. But hey, we gotta tell somebody."

"We'll tell Doc and Sarah. Maybe one of them will have an answer on how to handle this. But that's all we're going to tell." The Bentley purred down the interstate, then onto the two-lane, north and heading home.

On the down side of Albie Pass, Jud was reviewing his recent theorem hatched on the meadows of Carrie Creek about how a man's life is made up of equal parts: one part good luck, one part bad luck, and one part with no luck one way or the other—those forgettable and ordinary days. Penny's stay was the perfect proof to his theory: one day, his first day of great fishing and the good fortune to land a remarkable trout; his second day with the stomach flu, which surely qualifies as forgettable; and today when he was called home, the worst kind of luck.

"You know, Henry, I have a theory," he said pouring himself a scotch and one for Henry from the backseat bar. Henry could sense what was coming, having heard this tone in Jud's voice many times before. He settled down into the leather seat and raised his eyebrows in a fashion that read, "Here we go again—a Judson C. Clark diatribe." It couldn't be too long, thankfully, as Travers was only fifteen miles away.

"You see, the way I figure it, life is divided into thirds. . . ."

Afterword

AMAZING STORY, THAT last one, about Sir Gordon coming to Travers. Now, to find fourth generations, such as Jud and Henry, living in the same town their ancestors founded is not really that uncommon in rural Montana. That they are lifetime friends and fishermen makes the story only slightly harder to believe. But, to have Sir Gordon find them by accident; to join them; to fish the same waters together, waters their forefathers not only fished, but named—well that story, *that* story is just flat-out near impossible. Talk about coming full circle.

Jud, of course, has a theory about circles, but by now the reader has surely realized that Jud has a theory on just about everything. Jud's thinking is that life is a circle. Nothing profound there; all religions are based on a circle of sorts: life, death, life again; the divine three-sixty. Jud's philosophy on circles would have, quite naturally, his own spin on it. . . .

The Earth is an imperfect circle, traveling in an imperfect orbit, inhabited by one single, imperfect species. It's ironic that the one existing imperfect species is the only species, save one, capable of creating a perfect circle. With a string and a pencil, a compass, or a computer, man can make a perfect circle. But, he needs implements. He can't do it freehand.

To find the other perfect circle, a more natural and pure circle than man's tool-tainted efforts, you must journey to the quiet stretches, where on silken waters and windless evenings, the trout come to feed, rising short of the surface to sip the mayflies. The rise results in rings, at first a vortex; then liquid arches, radiating into flawless rings, ephemeral spheres of perfection; until the current catches them and washes them downstream.

It is inside these circles, in pursuit of trout, where Jud has found his greatest solace, his best of times. His theory looks on the rings as more than just the prime target of a pastime, but as more of a sign, a message made of rises by a perfect predator. The message sent, in perfect circles, always seemed perfectly clear to Jud. The rings were there not only because a trout was on the rise, but as a reminder; a reminder not to get lost in one circle and its perfection and forget about the perfection that encircles him. The perfection of being somewhere near Travers Corners and fully alive in the Elkheart, on a trout stream, where all the beauty ever dreamed of blends into the reasons for it all.

Catch and release—it's another one of those circles.

* * *

See you back in Travers Corners next time.